DRUMMER
BOY AT
BULL RUN

Bonnets and Bugles Series · 1

DRUMMER BOY AT BULL RUN

GILBERT MORRIS

MOODY PRESS
CHICAGO

ISBN: 0-8024-0911-3

5 7 9 10 8 6 4

Printed in the United States of America

*To Mike Haley, Jr.,
a chip off the old block!*

Contents

 1. Will You Hate Me If There's a War?   9
 2. The End of Something   18
 3. I Won't Let You Go Alone!   28
 4. A New Arrival   38
 5. Boy with a Baby   47
 6. The Sutlers   59
 7. Mr. Lincoln   72
 8. A New Recruit   83
 9. A Brand New Army   92
10. The Army Moves Out   101
11. A Sort of Holiday   113
12. There Stands Jackson Like a Stone Wall!   121
13. The Fires of Battle   130
14. A Visitor for the Lieutenant   141
15. General Stonewall Jackson   152
16. Back to Kentucky   163
17. We Just Have to Believe God   173

1

Will You Hate Me If There's a War?

Pineville, Kentucky, was so close to the state line that the Virginia mountains were clearly visible. The quiet little town had few celebrations. Usually the Fourth of July was the most important. However, on one cool day in March 1861 the streets were filled with people, music, and the sound of laughter. Fifty years earlier the village had been incorporated, and this celebration had been ordained to call attention to that time.

The day was raw and windy, but no one seemed to mind—least of all the pretty girl who was tugging urgently at the sleeve of a boy close to the square-dance platform.

"Come on, Jeff—we're old enough!"

Leah Carter was barely thirteen, but she'd been yearning to square dance with the grown-ups for a long time. Her honey-colored hair gleamed as the pale sun touched it, and the green dress she wore matched the color of her eyes. It was her best dress. She'd been hoping that Jeff Majors would tell her how pretty it was—but he had not.

"Aw, I don't know how." Jeff was tall for his fourteen years and had the blackest hair Leah had ever seen. He had black eyes too—and brows to match. He was wearing a pair of stiff new jeans, a red-and-brown checked shirt, and a pair of new

9

brown boots. Digging the toe of the right one into the dirt, he said stubbornly, "Anyway, your pa would paddle you if he caught you dancing."

"He would not!" Leah tossed her long hair. "He's never paddled me!"

Jeff suddenly grinned at her, his eyes crinkling until they were mere slits—they crinkled like his father's and brother's. "I can think of a time or two when he *should* have tanned you. Like the time you and Walter Beddows—"

"I don't want to hear about Walter Beddows!" Leah interrupted, her face turning pink. She hated Jeff's teasing. They'd grown up together, their families were the closest of friends, but for the last year she'd suddenly become aware of how handsome a boy Jeff was—though she'd never admit it. "Come on, I'll teach you."

Jeff tried to draw back, but she caught his arm and pulled him toward the low platform. The square dancers were moving to the music of a five-piece band, including two guitars, a banjo, a fiddle, and a dulcimer.

"I feel like a fool, Leah!" he protested. But somehow he found himself on the platform. He kept his eyes on his feet, trying to follow Leah's instructions. He knew he'd take a great deal of ribbing by his friends.

Right now he heard one of them calling, "Hey, Jeff! Where'd you get that pretty gal?"

"Don't pay any attention to that old Jay Walters!" Leah whispered. "You're doing fine!"

Two men arrived at the long refreshment table just then, and one squinted at the square dancers. He was six feet tall, and a fine black suit set off his trim figure. Nelson Majors had the same dark hair and eyes as his son Jeff. "Will you look at that, Daniel!" he exclaimed.

Daniel Carter was a smaller man than his friend, no more than five feet ten inches. His light brown hair was growing thin on the crown, and his eyes were a faded blue. His mouth was firm under a scraggly mustache, but there was a fragile quality in his features. A look of surprise swept over his face. "Why—that's Leah and Jeff!"

Nelson Majors laughed at the expression on his friend's face. "They're growing up fast."

"Not fast enough to start square dancing with the grown-ups, I don't reckon." Carter scowled. Then, in spite of himself, a grin touched his lips. "That girl! She's stubborn as a blue-nosed mule! I'll give her a thrashing when I get her home!"

"Be the first one, I reckon. Say, look at that." He grinned as his older son, Tom, approached the young couple. "He's going to tease the life out of Jeff for this stunt!'

Jeff, concentrating on his feet, jumped when a hand tapped his shoulder. He whirled around to find his brother standing there, a smile dancing in his dark eyes. "Cutting in on you, little brother," Tom announced cheerfully. He turned to Leah, adding, "I make it a habit to dance with every pretty girl."

Leah almost giggled, but decided that was not ladylike. Instead she let Tom Majors direct her around the floor. She caught a glimpse of Jeff stomping away—and then she did giggle. "He's mad at you."

"Do him good to be jealous." Tom smiled down at her. "I didn't think anybody on earth could make Jeff get up and dance in public. What'd you do, Leah—put a spell on him?"

11

"Oh, you just have to know how to handle Jeff." Leah nodded wisely. "He's shy, Mister Tom, but I know how to get him to do things."

"I'll bet you do!" A merry light gleamed in Tom Majors's eyes. "You've been bossing him around since you were six years old. What I want to know is, how—"

He broke off suddenly, as a shout caught their ears. "It's a fight!" he exclaimed. Releasing her, he dashed off the platform. Shouldering his way past a circle of men, Tom stared at the two young men who were pounding each other furiously.

The crowd was urging them on, but Tom instantly stepped between the two.

"Royal—Dave—!" He caught a wild blow on the cheek that drove his head back, but he yelled, "Stop this foolishness!"

Royal Carter's face was contorted with anger. "Get out of the way, Tom! I'm going to stomp him!" Royal was not tall, but he was muscular and strong. Blond-haired and blue-eyed, he tried to look older by wearing a large mustache and heavy sideburns. He was Tom's best friend.

"You ain't stompin' nobody, Carter!" Dave Mellon was much larger than his opponent but had taken several blows in the face. His lip was cut, and a large bruise was darkening on his cheek. His face was crimson with rage, and he tried to push Tom aside. "You taking up for him, Tom? You ought to know better!"

"What's all this?" Now Mr. Carter had arrived at the inner circle, followed by Nelson Majors. He took his son's arm. "Royal, you know better than to brawl in public!"

Ordinarily Royal Carter was a gentle young man—the last person one would expect to see in a fight. He was nineteen and had the nickname of "Professor" among his friends. Now he was pale with anger, and he glared at Mellon. "He cussed the president and the Union," Royal said. "I won't stand for that!"

"You and the rest of your Yankee friends will stand for more than that, Carter!" Dave Mellon was an outspoken abolitionist—which meant he was for freeing the slaves even if it meant war. President Lincoln would fight only to preserve the Union. "This country can't put up with slavery!"

An angry mutter ran around the crowd.

Mr. Carter glanced around. Mellon's words had divided the men into two groups. All were his neighbors, but they differed strongly on the matter of states' rights—and slavery.

It's the same all over this country, he thought sadly. *Men who've gotten along all their lives are ready to start shooting at each other!*

"Come along, Royal," he said quietly. He turned, and his son—giving one hard glance at Dave Mellon—obeyed. They pushed their way through the crowd.

A man said loudly, "Why don't you just go South, Carter?"

But Daniel Carter ignored him.

When the men reached the refreshment table, they found their wives waiting. "Are you all right, son?" Mary Carter was younger than her husband. She was a strong woman—which was very good, because Mr. Carter was not always well. "I thought you and Dave were good friends."

"Not anymore," Royal said sharply. "You should have heard what he said about us!"

13

"You're going to hear worse, Royal." Nelson Majors was very fond of young Carter. The young man had spent much time in his home over the years. Now worry disturbed Mr. Majors's dark eyes. "This business about slavery and states' rights isn't going to get any better."

"Do you think there'll be a war, Nelson?" The question was asked by his wife, Irene, a frail woman who wore a worried expression. In her youth, she had been a great beauty, but sickness had drained her, and now she looked frightened.

"I hope not," Mr. Majors said quickly. But his eyes met those of Daniel Carter—and he knew they were thinking the same thing.

"There'll have to be a war," Tom insisted. "The Yankees will force it on us."

"Why, you don't own any slaves, Tom," Royal said.

"No, and I never will. But a state has the right to decide for itself what to do!"

That was the real issue that faced the country —whether or not a state could leave the Union if it so decided. And though the two families said no more, the celebration was spoiled for them.

They all seemed to realize that the lifelong friendship between the Carters and the Majors family was in peril. Indeed, the United States of America was on the verge of disaster.

* * *

"Oh, Jeff, it's the wren's egg—the one we've looked for for so long!" Leah held the tiny blue egg in her hand. Her face was alive with pleasure.

Leah and Jeff were high in a towering sycamore tree. They'd become expert tree climbers in

14

their joint determination to collect a specimen of every bird's egg in the county. Leah was wearing her old overalls, and the two sat as easily on the limb as if it had been a solid bench.

"I was about to give up." Jeff stared down at the blue egg with satisfaction. "Well, now we can add this one—but we still don't have one from a woodpecker."

Leah began to count off the eggs they still needed to find. She had not gotten through the list, however, when the sound of horses approaching made her break off.

"Let's get down," she said hurriedly. "We'll look silly up in this old tree!"

"Too late," Jeff said. "They'll pass by us."

But the tree where they'd found the wren's nest was beside the road, and the road crossed a large brook at the same spot. Most riders paused there to water their horses, and this was exactly what happened.

"It's your brother!" Leah whispered in alarm.

"And that's your sister with him!" Jeff wanted to get away, but the buggy his brother drove came to a stop beneath their tree.

"We'll water the team," Tom said. "It's been a thirsty drive."

"Well, all right, but then you'll have to take me home, Tom."

Leah stared down through the foliage but could see only the top of the buggy. She could hear them, however, and she whispered, "We can't eavesdrop on them!"

"Cover your ears, then!" Jeff whispered back. "We can't let them see us up here!" He wished he were up any other tree in the world.

15

"Sarah, you know I love you," Tom said. "And I thought you cared for me."

"Oh, Tom!" Sarah Carter was a beautiful girl. She had blonde hair, dark blue eyes, and a creamy complexion. Her simple blue dress set off her trim figure, and she was highly sought after by several young men. But her eyes were troubled as she said, "We can't even talk about things like that."

"Why not?" Tom demanded.

"Because things are so—so confused." Sarah bit her lip. "There may be war next week. You know that, Tom."

"Why, there's always something for people to worry about. If people waited until there were no problems, nobody would ever get married!"

"This is different, Tom, and you know it." Sarah went on, speaking softly but pointing out the difficulties. She ended by saying, "If war comes, you'd fight for the Union, wouldn't you, Tom?"

"I—I guess I'd have to, Sarah."

"And my brother Royal would fight for the South." Worry crossed her smooth face, and she asked suddenly, "What would it be like if I married you—and you killed my brother—or if he killed you? Don't you see how terrible that would be?"

Tom could only ask her to change her mind. Finally he said heavily, "I guess all we can do is hope there's no war."

Then he spoke to the horses, and the buggy pulled away.

Leah waited until she could not hear the sound of the horses and wheels, then climbed down the tree.

Jeff slid to the ground too, keeping his eyes fixed on the buggy, which was turning past a distant grove of trees. "I wish we hadn't been up in that tree," he muttered.

"You knew he was courting her. Everybody knows that."

"Yeah, but I feel guilty about listening to them. That wasn't right!"

"I know. I feel the same way—but we couldn't help it." She put the tiny egg into a small box lined with cotton and closed the lid. The pleasure of the hunt was gone now, and she said, "I've got to get home."

"Me too."

They plodded along silently, each thinking of what they had heard. But when they came to the fork that led to the Carter place, Leah stopped abruptly and looked into his eyes. "Jeff—will you hate me if there's a war?"

"Why . . . that's a crazy thing to say!" Jeff blurted out. "Of course not!"

Leah studied his face for a moment, then whispered, "I'd never hate you, Jeff, no matter what!" There was a catch in her voice, and she whirled and dashed down the road.

Jeff watched her go. He almost ran after her. Then he thought of what Tom and Sarah had said. He whispered, "I'll never hate you, Leah—not ever!"

Then he resumed his slow walk toward his house. His shoulders were slumped, and his dark eyes were filled with doubt. A woodpecker drummed on a dead pine over his head, but young Jeff Majors was so troubled with thoughts of a war that he did not even glance up.

2
The End of Something

For many years people remembered what a fine spring Kentucky enjoyed in 1861. Perhaps the dread of war, which cast gloom over the state, made the skies seem more blue and the dogwood whiter. March with its gusty winds faded, and April brought warm, gentle breezes that seemed to draw the tiny green tongues of crocuses out of the dead clods.

Leah always remembered it as a golden time. She and Jeff ranged the woods, hunting—he for rabbits and squirrels, she for birds' eggs. She never forgot how the tiny buds softened the trees that lined the river bottoms or how the wild violets turned the ground into a fine lavender carpet. It was a spring to be remembered!

On one of their jaunts, they were returning home after a long afternoon in the woods. The sun was dipping behind the foothills in the west, and Leah murmured wistfully, "I wish we could do this every day!"

Jeff turned to grin at her. "We'd get mighty hungry, I reckon. Somebody's got to do the work." He hefted his bag in his left hand. "I like squirrel and dumplings—but not all the time."

"Oh, you're always so—so practical, Jeff Majors!"

"Somebody has to be. You can't eat birds' eggs and that poetry you like so much." He trudged on a few paces. "Spring plowing tomorrow. No more days like this for a while."

Leah had put aside the memory of the time in the sycamore tree. Tom still came to sit on the Carter porch, but something had been lost. She could not say what it was, but there was a lack of joy in Tom and Sarah now.

"Maybe we can go hunting on Sunday afternoon," she said hopefully. These days in the woods with Jeff were the best times for her, and she hated to think they were ending.

"Not likely your pa would let you do it. You know how strict he is on the Sabbath." Jeff grinned again. "I don't reckon he'd eat an egg laid on Sunday!"

They came to the small wooden bridge that spanned the creek and, as usual, stopped to lean on the rail. The western sky was red, and the water below reflected the hue.

Suddenly Leah stiffened. "Look—there he is, Jeff!"

Jeff followed her gesture and whispered, "It's Old Napoleon!" He stared at the huge bass. It rose to take a mayfly and then sank back into the depths. "Wish I'd brought my fishin' pole! I'd get him!"

The large fish had eluded Jeff's efforts for months. Leah knew the boy had tried every bait and every time of day and night—all to no avail.

"Let's go get the poles at our house and come back. Maybe we'll get him." Leah didn't care about Old Napoleon—so named for his craftiness—but she longed to make the day last longer.

"All right. But your pa won't stand for it."

"I'll talk him into it. Come on, Jeff!"

19

The two broke into a run, turning off at the lane that led to the Carter house. They grabbed the poles that leaned against a shed, but as they were raking bait out of the worm box, Leah's father stepped around the corner.

"What are you two doing?"

"Oh, Pa!" Leah held up a huge night crawler that wiggled frantically in her grasp. "We just saw Old Napoleon at the bridge. Jeff and me are going back to catch him!"

"Why, it'll be dark by the time you get back!"

"I don't care, Pa!"

"Your mother's about got supper on the table, Leah. You know how it frets her when anybody's late to a meal."

"Pa, we may never get another chance at that old Napoleon!"

Daniel Carter stood silently in the fading twilight, his face stiff and his shoulders stooping.

Leah looked up at him with a startled expression. "Pa . . . is something wrong? Are you sick?" She was well aware of her father's poor health, and in the dusk he looked weak and frail.

"No, I'm not sick. But bad news has come."

"Bad news?"

"Yes, Leah . . . very bad news."

Jeff shifted awkwardly, as if he felt he was intruding into private affairs. "Well, I'll just be moseying home . . ."

Mr. Carter turned his gaze on the boy. "It's bad news for all of us, Jeff. For your family too."

"What is it, Pa? Is it the war? Is that it, Pa?"

"Yes, Leah."

Leah felt a coldness in her stomach, and fear ran along her nerves. Though the threat of war had lain over them for a long time, somehow she had always thought that it would never really come. Though she'd heard the grown-ups talking about it, it had seemed like something far off. Now it was here.

She moved to her father's side and took his hand. "Is it certain, Pa?"

"I'm afraid so, Leah. News just came today. It started in South Carolina. There's a fort just offshore—Fort Sumter, it's called. There were Union soldiers there—and the Southern forces began shelling it."

Jeff spoke up quickly. "Maybe the North will let the South be a different country, Mr. Carter."

Daniel Carter shook his head. "No, Jeff. President Lincoln has made it plain that he can tolerate slavery but that he won't stand for secession. It's his view that the Union must be held together."

Jeff stared, then muttered, "Guess I better get home, sir." He whirled and ran out of the yard, his lean form fading into the gathering darkness.

Leah watched him go, and a great sadness came over her. "Will Royal go to the war, Pa?"

"I expect he will, Leah." Her father stared after Jeff, then murmured, "And Tom Majors will go too. And that will break Sarah's heart!"

* * *

The dining room seemed to have become smaller, for it held not only all of the Carters but the Nelson Majors family as well. For years the two families had entertained each other, and as Mr. Carter looked around the crowded table, he said, "We haven't done this in a long time, Nelson. I've missed it."

21

Jeff's father looked down the table at Mrs. Carter. "I remember every meal I've ever had here, Mary. You're the second-best cook in the world!" Reaching out, he clasped his wife's hand and smiled. "No offense, but I've got to live with this woman for a long time. Pays to keep on the good side of her."

Jeff's mother was expecting a child, and she had not been well. She had eaten almost nothing, and her face was pale and drawn. But with an effort she smiled at her husband. "You'd do anything to get a chocolate cake out of me, Nelson!"

A laugh ran around the table.

Tom said, "Dad's not afraid of anybody—except my mother!" He was sitting across from Sarah, and Leah had noticed that the two of them had hardly spoken.

Then Tom looked across at Royal and said, "Well, Professor, when do you go back to college?" He grinned, adding, "In my opinion, you've been educated beyond your capacity!"

Royal looked up with a faint smile but said only, "My teachers would probably agree with you."

The meal went on, and then all of the women helped to clear the table. They returned from the kitchen carrying huge chunks of apple pie and steaming cups of coffee.

Leah set the largest before Jeff, whispering, "If you eat all that, you'll probably die!"

"I'll risk it." Jeff dug his fork into the hot dessert. When his mouth was full, he said, "This is good, Miz Carter!"

His father laughed. "Why, Jeff, the worst piece of pie you ever had was good. You never taste anything, I don't think. Now slow down and show some manners!"

"Let the lad be, Nelson." Daniel Carter smiled. "I remember how I ate the same way when I was his age." His blue eyes grew soft. "I would go out into the garden and dig up a big white onion, hot as fire! And I'd just eat it like it was an apple." He stared down at his small slice of pie and shook his head sadly. "Only a boy can eat like that."

"I eat onions like that!" Royal exclaimed.

"I'd rather have this pie than an old onion," Leah piped up. Apple pie dribbled down her lip, but before her mother could rebuke her, she dabbed at it with her napkin.

The talk ran around the table. Only Morena Carter said nothing. She was a beautiful girl of eight but had never spoken. She had a sweet expression on her face—but somehow it was blank.

Leah reached out and fed her from time to time, spearing a fragrant piece of apple on a fork. Morena ate it daintily with a smile. She would never grow any older mentally, Leah understood, but she loved her little sister with a fierce devotion.

Her mother sat talking quietly to Mrs. Majors, speaking about the child that was to come. She was very concerned, for Irene Majors was somewhat old to be bearing a child. Mary remembered the hard time that Irene had gone through when Jeff was born—and she knew that Dr. Kinsman had advised her not to have more children.

"We'll have that baby of yours dressed up like a prince, Irene—or a princess." Mrs. Majors smiled. "I've still got some of that fine silk Daniel brought in from Lexington."

Jeff's father was listening, and something came into his face. "I guess you won't be able to help with the baby, Mary," he said quietly.

The talk that had been humming fell off, and Mr. Majors stared down at his coffee. When he looked up, his jaw was set, and Leah could see that he was unhappy. "It's good of you to offer—but we won't be here."

"Won't be here?" her father echoed. "Why—you're not leaving, Nelson?"

"Yes, we're moving." He glanced at his wife and nodded. "We've sold our place—and we're moving to Richmond."

His words sent a chill through Leah. She twisted her head to look at Jeff—but he kept his eyes on the table.

Royal said, "I don't think that's wise, sir."

"I agree," her father spoke up at once. "I've been afraid of something like this. It's the war, of course—but the South can't win. Why, they have no army, no munitions factory, no navy! It can't survive. I see your mind is made up, but wait for six months, Nelson!"

"I know you mean well, Dan—" Jeff's father shrugged "—but Irene and I are agreed. You know Virginia's our home."

"Yes, and Nelson went to West Point. He was trained as an officer in the engineers, you know." Mrs. Majors's face was pale, but she said, "It's got to be."

"Irene, stay here with us—just until the baby is born," Leah's mother urged. "Then we'll take you to Richmond."

"No, I'll go with my family—but it's kind of you to offer, Mary."

Royal looked across the table toward Tom. "You'll be going too?"

24

"Yes. I'll go with the South, Royal—just as you'll go with the North."

The cheer had gone out of the room, and it was Jeff's father who finally said, "We've been close— very close. I don't reckon we could think more highly of anybody than we do of you folks. But we've got to go. I heard that General Scott offered to make Robert E. Lee commander of the whole Union army. But Lee said he had to go with his state—which is Virginia. I've got to do the same thing, Dan."

After the Majors family had left, Leah came to sit close to her father. "Do they *have* to go, Pa?" she asked plaintively.

He reached over and pulled her close. "I guess they do, Pet," he answered, calling her by her baby nickname. "And I guess all over the country families are being divided—friends are saying good-bye."

"I hate it, Pa!"

"So do I—but God will see us through it!"

* * *

"Sarah, come with me!"

"Oh, Tom, you know I can't!"

Sarah stood beside the towering pine tree that shadowed the family's small herd of milk cows. Tom knew her habits well enough to have found her. She'd been startled when he'd suddenly appeared. And she'd known at once why he'd come.

He put his hands on her shoulders. "I love you so much, Sarah! Come with me to Virginia. We'll get married—"

"No, Tom." Sarah could not meet his eyes, for the longing she saw there was a reflection of her own feelings. "You know it's impossible."

Tom argued for half an hour but finally said heavily, "I guess I knew it was hopeless—but I had to try."

"When will you be leaving?"

"Next week." He suddenly took her in his arms and kissed her. "Wait for me, Sarah!"

And then he wheeled and ran to where he'd tied his horse.

Sarah watched him go, wondering if she'd ever see him again.

* * *

Jeff had known he'd have to say good-bye to Leah. "Pa, you all go on. I'll catch up to you."

Nelson Majors looked down. It was clear that he understood the misery in the boy. "All right. Tell her good-bye for all of us, son."

Jeff mounted the roan mare and rode out of the yard. His mother was already in the wagon, and Tom was driving the second team. Everything had been sold except what was in those two wagons, and a sense of loss came over him as he left. This was the only home he'd known, and he hated the idea of leaving.

He galloped the mare, his head down, and when he arrived at the Carter place he saw Leah working in the garden.

When she saw him, she dropped her hoe and ran to meet him.

As Jeff slipped off the mare, he saw that she was close to crying. "I—I just came to say good-bye," he muttered.

Leah swallowed hard, her voice unsteady as she whispered, "You promised to write me, Jeff."

"Sure—and you've got to write back."

26

"I will—I promise."

Then they just stood there awkwardly.

Finally Leah cried in a forlorn voice, "Oh, Jeff! I won't have a friend!"

"Course you will!"

"Not like you!"

Jeff knew he had to go—or act like a baby! "Good-bye, Leah," he whispered hoarsely.

He ducked his head, meaning to leave—but Leah abruptly threw her arms around him. She was crying hard now, and her fingers dug into his back.

Jeff blinked hard, patting her clumsily on the shoulder. Then he pulled away and mounted his horse. As he rode down the trail he heard Leah crying after him, "Jeff! Jeff!"

When he was out of sight, he drew his sleeve fiercely across his eyes and clamped his teeth together. "Good-bye, Leah!" he muttered, then kicked the startled horse into a dead run.

Later that day the Majorses' two wagons crossed a rise, then came to a halt. Jeff's father said heavily, "Well, there's Virginia."

Jeff stared at the hills that rose in front of them but said nothing. Glancing at Tom, he noted that his brother's face was gloomy.

His mother said, probably as cheerfully as she could, "Well, it's hard to leave Kentucky—but Virginia's our home now."

"So it is, Irene." His father spoke to the team, and they moved forward.

Soon they passed down into the valley and on to the green foothills of Virginia.

3

I Won't Let You Go Alone!

Leah, there's no sense moping around like a sick kitten," Mrs. Carter said sharply. She was hanging out the washing, and the wind puffed the dresses and shirts so that they danced in the stiff breeze. "Jeff is gone, and you might as well get used to it."

Leah draped a pair of Royal's long underwear over the line before she said, "Oh, Ma, there's nothing to do now that he's gone!"

"There's plenty of work to do, young lady—" Leah's mother broke off as Mr. Carter emerged from the house. "Well, now you have something to do. You can go to town with your father. Be sure you get everything I put on the grocery list." She frowned, adding, "Don't expect him to help. He's so fired up over this war he can't remember to tie his shoes!"

"Come along, daughter. We've got to be on our way."

"All right, Pa." Leah hurried to the barn and helped her father hitch the team to the buggy. "Let me drive," she begged, and when he agreed, she leaped into the seat. "Hold on now," she commanded, then sent the horses out of the yard at a sprightly pace.

Leah loved horses, and her father had taught her to drive when she was barely able to hold the lines.

Now as they sped along, he gave her a fond glance, thinking, *She's a fine girl—none better any-*

28

where! He admired her smooth, rosy cheeks and her blonde hair, escaping the edges of her bonnet. *Thirteen years old—she'll be a woman soon.*

Aloud he said, "You miss Jeff pretty bad, don't you, Pet?"

Leah kept her eyes on the shiny coats of the horses. "Oh, I guess so . . ."

Mr. Carter knew his daughter very well. She was not a great talker about how she felt—but he knew that she had been lonely since the boy had gone.

"Well," he said finally, "I miss Jeff. I miss them all. Didn't know how much I thought of the Majors family until they were gone."

Eagerly Leah turned to face him, her green eyes bright with hope. "Do you think they'll come back here to live—when the war's over, I mean?"

"That might be a long time, I'm afraid."

"But everybody says the Rebels will be whipped in six months!"

"Everybody is probably wrong, Pet." A sorrowful light came to her father's faded blue eyes. His thin shoulders were sharply outlined under his worn blue-and-white checked shirt. "The Confederates are fighting for their homes. They're not likely to give up easily."

The iron-shod hooves of the team struck rhythmically on the dirt road, sending up clouds of fine dust behind the buggy.

Leah said nothing for five minutes, then she whispered, "Pa . . . I'm afraid something will happen to Royal . . . and to Jeff . . . and his family."

"I'm afraid too," her father said simply. "But we'll have to pray that they will be safe."

29

Mr. Carter had always been able to talk to Leah, even more than he had with Royal. The love between the two of them ran deep, and as the buggy rolled down the dusty road, he tried to calm her fears.

As they approached the town, he said with surprise, "Why, look at that, Pet!"

Leah glanced down the road. "Why, Pa, it looks like everybody in the county is in town! And it's not even a Saturday!"

The streets of Pineville were so packed with wagons and horses that Leah had to drive all the way to the blacksmith shop on the far end of the main street.

Clyde Potter, the blacksmith, came out to greet them.

Her father asked, "What in the world is going on, Clyde?"

"Why, it's the army, come to recruit, Daniel," the big man responded. He shook his head. "Never seen nothing like it! Everybody's here, and it looks like every young feller in the county is bound to get into this here war!"

Mr. Carter got down slowly and gazed at the milling crowd in the square. "Are they recruiting for the Union—or for the South?"

Potter gave him a sharp glance. Tempers were short, for Kentucky had not come out for either side. "Well, Kentucky is a border state, you know"—one of the states that lay between the North and the South.

"I guess there's more Union sentiment here, Clyde."

"Well, reckon that's right," the blacksmith admitted. "I'm Union myself, and I reckoned you was too." He waved his brawny arm toward the west. "There was a feller from Virginia over to Ripley three days ago. Lots of Southern sympathizers in that part of the state. I guess the Rebs did their recruiting there. Feller who's come to raise a company for the Union is Silas Bates. He's from Kentucky, but he's raising a company called the Washington Blues."

Mr. Carter understood at once. "Both the North and the South want Kentucky to come with them. But until this state comes out openly, both sides will be recruiting our men to fight."

"Pa, let's go watch!" Leah begged.

"Guess we will, Pet." He asked the blacksmith to replace a shoe on one of the horses, then the two moved toward the square.

It was so crowded that they could not get close to the platform where the mayor and several other town leaders were sitting. Finally they found a place to one side where they could see, and as soon as they were settled a band began to play.

For the next hour the square was filled with music and then a speech by the mayor. None of it interested Leah much, but when Mayor Buckley introduced a tall man dressed in an immaculate uniform, she grew more attentive.

". . . and now, I introduce to you Major Silas Bates!"

Major Bates—wearing a saber with a glittering hilt—was greeted with wild applause. He held up his hand for silence, then began to speak in a powerful voice. "I come to give a call to action! The rebellion has begun, and all good men of the North must answer that call . . ."

He spoke with enthusiasm, and when he was finished, he cried out, "Which of you young men will join in our noble cause? Do you have a soul to free the slaves from their shackles of bondage?"

Loud cries arose, and Major Bates looked at the crowd with satisfaction.

"My sergeant is here to enlist you. Your tour of duty will be for ninety days—and by that time we'll have crushed the Rebels into the dust!"

Leah watched as a line formed instantly, and she said, "Look, Pa! It's Royal!"

Mr. Carter had seen his son earlier and had known this would happen. He said nothing.

Royal finally turned from the recruiting table, his face flushed with excitement. When he saw his father and sister, he came to them at once. "I wanted to talk to you before I joined, Pa," he faltered. "But you knew this was coming, I think."

"Yes, Royal. Now you must be the best soldier you can. It won't be easy in the army, but you'll have Jesus with you."

Royal was obviously relieved. "I'm glad you understand, Pa," he said. "Now, sister, let's go get some of those refreshments Major Bates has furnished!"

All over the land the scene that had occurred at Pineville was duplicated. Young men rushed to enlist—most of them fearing that the war would be over before they could see action.

President Lincoln called for 75,000 volunteers for three months. In the streets of the large cities, men surged to the colors. The whole North rose as one man.

Everywhere the drum and fife thrilled the air with their stirring call. Hastily formed companies marched to camps, and the measured tread of soldiers filled the land.

And as it was in the North, so it was in the South. Four more states joined the Confederacy—Virginia, Arkansas, North Carolina, and Tennessee.

From the mountains and valleys of the South came a shout of fierce resolve to capture Washington, the capital of the North. Plowboys left their mules in the field, and clerks forsook their ledgers to join the newly formed companies that were organized daily.

And in both North and South, war preparations were made in a holiday atmosphere. Both sides were confident of victory, and neither had any idea of the terrible bloodshed that lay ahead.

Almost no one stopped to think that thousands of the strong young men who rushed to join the two armies would lie in shallow graves before the year was out.

* * *

"Ma—what's wrong with Pa?"

Leah and Mrs. Carter were sitting on the front porch. Her mother had been reading aloud from the Bible, but Leah had not been able to pay attention.

Mrs. Carter looked up with surprise, then slowly closed the worn Book.

Leah shook her head. "He's worried all the time —and he's gone so much."

"He's troubled, Leah. He feels useless because he can't do anything to help."

"With the war, Ma?"

"Yes." Running her hand over the leather cover of the Bible, her mother added, "All the young men

33

are gone to fight, but your pa's too old to do that—and he's not well."

"He shouldn't feel bad," Leah insisted. "None of the other older men are going."

"Your pa's always wanted to be helpful. Now he can't—and it's hurting him."

Leah said no more, but two days later her father had an announcement for the family. They were seated at the table, and when the meal was over he said, "I've got something to tell you."

Leah was feeding Morena, and in the sudden silence the little girl looked around, her eyes going from face to face. Sarah had half risen to start clearing the table, but she sat down again when she saw her father's face. "What is it, Pa?" she asked.

Clearing his throat, Mr. Carter said slowly, "I guess you've all noticed that I've been troubled lately."

"You've been feeling poorly, Daniel," his wife said quickly.

"It's not that. I've been feeling called to do something—but I couldn't see what it was." Taking a deep breath, he looked around the table, studying each face. "Now I know what I've got to do."

Mrs. Carter stared at her husband fearfully.

He seemed to read her thoughts. "I'm too old to join the army," he said, "but I'm not too old to help the soldiers."

"Help them how?"

"I'm going to be a sutler."

Leah piped up. "What's a sutler, Pa?"

"The army has to have supplies, Leah," he said. "The army takes care of equipment such as muskets and uniforms—but the soldiers need personal

34

things." His face grew bright as he explained. "Sutlers follow the army with wagons filled with things the soldiers need—paper to write letters on, needles and thread, candy—things like that."

At once Leah's mother said, "Why, Daniel Carter, you can't mean to become a traveling peddler!"

"Well, it's more than that, Mary." He paused, then said, "The soldiers need more than candy and paper. What I'm going to do is carry tracts and Bibles along with the other supplies. Those young men need the gospel—the Word of God. And I'm going to see that they get it!"

Instantly Mrs. Carter and Sarah began to argue with him. They thought he was not fitted to endure the hardships of such a life. "Why, you wouldn't last a month, Pa!" Sarah exclaimed. "You'd get sick, and who'd take care of you?"

He listened as the two spoke but finally said, "I know you're right about my being in poor shape. But I feel that God has called me to do this thing— and when God commands a thing, He'll take care of those who obey."

That was just the beginning of the matter, however. For the next two weeks the house was filled with strain. Leah's father began at once to prepare for his new "mission," as he called it. He hired extra help for the farm and made arrangements for the crops. He spent considerable time buying a wagon and having a carpenter convert it into a sutler's wagon.

Leah watched this being done and was fascinated by the shelves and the bed that fitted cleverly inside. She was aware that her mother and sister were opposed to everything about her father's idea, but she was intrigued with it.

Finally the wagon was finished, and Leah accompanied her father to the county seat to buy supplies. They had to camp overnight beside a stream, and she cooked supper over a campfire.

As her father ate the last of the stew she'd made, he glanced at her with a smile. "Pet, you're a fine cook! I wish I could take you with me."

Leah took a deep breath. "Pa, I *am* going with you!"

He stared at her, then laughed. "Why, you can't do that—though I wish you could."

"If God's going to take care of you, He'll take care of me too." She came over and sat beside him. Picking up his hand, she held it in both of hers. "Pa, all my life I've heard you tell how the Lord told you to do something or other. I never understood—because He never said anything to me."

"He will when you—"

"Pa, I'm trying to tell you—God's been telling me to go with you."

"Oh, Pet, you just want to go!"

"Yes, I do—but ever since you told us what you were going to do, something's been happening to me." The firelight was reflected in her eyes, and she struggled with what was inside her. "I . . . I've been waking up every night, Pa," she whispered. "And all I could think of was going with you! It's not like anything *I* would think of—it must be something God wants me to do. I won't let you go alone!"

He sat very still, his hand held by her strong hands. He listened as she spoke, and finally he said, "I don't know, daughter . . ."

The two of them sat there for a long time, not speaking. Finally he hugged her, saying, "I'll pray on it—and your mother will have to pray with me."

When they arrived back at the farm, he warned Leah, "Say nothing to your ma about this thing, Pet. Not yet."

"No, Pa."

For the next two days Leah almost ached with anxiety. Her father said nothing, and her mother did not mention the matter. Leah could see that both of them were troubled, and she became convinced that there was no hope. Her father was due to leave soon, and when the days passed without a word, Leah cried bitter tears into her pillow.

Early one morning, Leah's mother came to her room. She had been crying, Leah saw at once.

"Leah, your father and I have agreed." She put her arm around Leah and kissed her. "We agree that it's God's will for you to go on this trip—"

"Oh, Ma!" Leah hugged her mother, and the two of them talked for a long time. "Ma, I'll take care of him," the girl said earnestly.

"I know you will, Leah," Mary Carter said gently. She stroked her daughter's fine blonde hair. "God has convinced me that He wants you with him just for that."

4

A New Arrival

Richmond was like a swarming hive of bees—or so it seemed to Jeff. All day the streets were packed with men and women intent on building an army. Officers shouldered their way through the crowds, and their dashing uniforms added color to the scene. To young Jeff Majors, moving from the placid farm in Kentucky to Richmond was like nothing he'd ever known.

Dodging between a pair of colonels dressed in gray, he muttered, "'Scuse me!" then darted out into the street. It was filled with buggies, saddle horses, and wagons loaded with all manner of freight but was less crowded than the sidewalks that ran in front of the shops.

I wish Leah could see all this! The thought of the girl brought a moment's sadness to him, for, despite the furious activities of Richmond, he missed Leah Carter.

Putting the thought behind him, he walked rapidly, arriving finally at a hardware store with a wooden stairway that led to a second story.

Jeff glanced at the small sign that said DR. HARTLEY BOWDEN and bounded up to the second floor. Entering the office, he saw that the worn chairs were filled with waiting patients—all men except for one middle-aged woman. *Good grief! I'll never get to see the doctor—not with this crowd!*

However, as he stood there the inner door opened, and a short, elderly man stepped out. He glared at Jeff through a pair of thick spectacles, then asked sharply, "Well, Jeff, what is it?"

Jeff glanced around the room, embarrassed by the stares of the patients. "Well—it's my ma, Doctor Bowden. She's poorly."

"Have her come in."

"I—I don't think she'll be able to do that, sir."

Dr. Bowden stared at the boy, his sharp black eyes intent. "Very well. I'll be there in two hours."

"Thank you, Doctor!"

Jeff wheeled and raced out of the office. He cleared the steps three at a time.

Reaching the street, he hesitated for one moment, then turned left and made his way toward the edge of town. The shops gave way to small factories, then to houses, and finally to more or less open country.

Jeff moved faster as he ran toward the mass of tents that dotted the landscape, and soon he was in the heart of the major encampment of the Confederate Army.

The camp seemed even busier than Richmond itself. Thousands of men milled around drill fields, horse-drawn cannons stirred huge clouds of dust, aides rushed through the camp with messages. Jeff loved it all!

As he made his way to his father's company, he was conscious of sergeants barking orders like yapping dogs, and the rattle of musket fire from the rifle range. Voices came to him—the soft slur of Southern voices peppered with French from a ragtag Louisiana unit. The air was thick with smells—

cooking meat, dust, horses, cattle, and always the acrid odor of latrines.

When Jeff reached the large tent that served as regimental headquarters, he saw his father standing with another officer in front of a tall table. He stopped abruptly and waited, and soon his father looked up and saw him. "Jeff—come over here."

When Jeff came up to the two men, his father said, "General, my son Jeff. Jeff, this is Colonel Jackson."

The colonel wore a forage cap pulled down low on his brow. He had the palest blue eyes Jeff had ever seen.

"I'm glad to meet you, Jeff," he said, extending his hand.

Jeff stammered, "And I'm glad to meet you, sir."

"I was with your father in West Point—did you know that?"

"Yes, sir! He told me."

"Jeff, what are you doing here?"

"Well, sir, it's Ma. She's—not doing well. I went by and asked Dr. Bowden to come. Was that all right?"

"Yes, it was. Colonel Jackson, could I have permission to go to my wife?"

"Of course, Lieutenant." Jackson nodded. "And I will pray with you that she will be touched with the healing hand of God."

"Thank you, Colonel! Jeff, come along."

Jeff followed his father to the corral, where he borrowed a horse. Jeff swung up behind, and the lieutenant kicked the horse into a fast gallop.

They said little, but Jeff asked once, "Is Ma going to be all right, Pa?"

"I pray she will, Jeff."

The answer gave him little comfort.

When they reached the tiny frame house, he waited outside. Pacing up and down nervously, he tried to convince himself that his mother would be all right. But a nagging fear kept gnawing at him.

Finally Dr. Bowden drove up in his buggy, and Jeff ran to hold the team. "My father's here now, Doctor."

Doctor Bowden grunted his thanks and disappeared into the house.

Jeff stroked the noses of the horses, then went to get some water in a pail. As the animals drank thirstily, he could not help worrying about his mother. She'd been sick ever since they'd left Kentucky. *She'll be all right after the baby comes*, he told himself and finally went to sit on the small porch.

Time seemed to drag. At last his father came out. There was a tense look on his face, and he said, "Jeff, your mother's not doing well. I want you to go bring Tom back. He'll have to get permission, but I've written a note. Give it to Major Greer. Take the horse."

"Yes, sir." As Jeff took the note he noticed that his father's lips were drawn into a tight line. "What did the doctor say, Pa?"

"He said that your mother—is not doing well. But we'll pray that she'll be better. Now, go get Tom!"

Jeff ran to the horse, swung into the saddle, then galloped down the road.

When he found his brother, Tom was eating supper.

"Tom, Pa says for you to come. Here's a note for Major Greer."

"Is it Ma, Jeff?"

"She's—she's doing real bad, Tom."

Major Greer readily granted permission, and the two made their way back to the house. As they reached the porch, the door opened, and Nelson Majors stepped outside. "Your mother . . ."

When his father paused, Jeff whispered, "Is she dead, Pa!"

"No—but the doctor fears she won't live."

It was the longest night of Jeff's life—and his brother and father suffered as well. They sat outside on the porch, hoping that the doctor was wrong, but when Doctor Bowden came outside just before dawn, he said quietly, "The child is here—a little girl."

"My wife?" Lieutenant Majors demanded.

Doctor Bowden hesitated, then shook his head. "She's very weak. You'd better go in to her."

The three of them moved inside and into the bedroom. Jeff saw the baby his mother held in her arms, and then his father fell to his knees beside her. "Irene . . ." he whispered.

"Nelson . . ." Her voice was very faint, and her face was pale as chalk. "We have . . . a little girl . . ."

"Yes! She's beautiful—just like you!"

"Her name is . . . Esther." Then she looked up and saw her boys. "Tom—Jeff."

They came to her, and she reached out a thin hand. "Take care of your . . . little sister . . . promise me!"

"We will, Ma!" Jeff could not see for the tears that burned in his eyes. He held his mother's hand.

For a time she spoke with them. They waited helplessly as she began to slip away, and finally she said, "I'm going to be with Jesus. I'll meet you all in heaven . . ."

Ten minutes later Jeff saw her eyes close and knew that she was gone. He looked at the baby, which his father now picked up. "We'll take care of her, Ma!" he whispered.

* * *

The funeral took place the next day—and the struggle to care for a newborn child began at once.

Esther was left temporarily with Mrs. Rena Barlow, the wife of C Company's sergeant. Her own baby had been born only a week earlier, and she'd said, "Just leave her with me, Lieutenant. I'll be glad to take care of her."

After the funeral, they went back to the small house, and the three of them sat around the table. All were in a state of shock, but something had to be done.

"How are we going to take care of her, Pa?" Tom asked his father.

"I don't know, Tom." Lieutenant Majors was haggard and could not seem to think. "We can leave her with Mrs. Barlow for a while."

"But not for long," Tom said. "Sooner or later the army will go to fight. What will happen then?"

"I just don't know, Tom," his father said. "We'll have to pray that God will open a way."

A week went by, and Jeff did all he could. His father and brother were drilling hard, for a battle was shaping up and their officers were demanding. Jeff spent time with Esther at the Barlows' house, and he quickly learned to care for her. She was a healthy baby and slept most of the time.

Every time his father came home, Jeff saw that he was under more strain.

"I wish I had brothers or sisters, but I don't," he told Jeff. "Your mother didn't either. We don't have any close kin to send her to."

Jeff could not get that out of his mind, and one night he stayed awake thinking for a long time. When he was almost asleep, an idea seemed to jump into his head. At once he sat upright, his mind working.

The next day he wrote a letter, posted it, then waited for several days. *I guess it was a crazy thing to do*, he told himself, *but we've got to do something!*

Almost a week later Jeff's father came to the Barlows', where Jeff was taking care of Esther. Jeff was surprised to see him. Then he saw a strange look on his father's face and asked, "Is something wrong, Pa?"

Nelson Majors looked at his son—then at his baby daughter. His face softened, and he took the child. For a moment he looked down into the small face, then he looked at his son.

"I got a letter from Mary Carter, Jeff."

"You—you did?" Jeff gulped. He looked down nervously. "Did she tell you I wrote her?"

"Yes. You should have talked to me first."

"I guess I know that, Pa. I'm sorry. But I was so worried about Esther—"

"I know, son." Taking a sheet of paper from his pocket, his father said, "Let me read you the letter."

Dear Nelson,

We received the sad news of Irene's death in a letter from Jeff. It must be terrible for you all, and we grieve with you. Irene was precious to all of

44

us. We loved her dearly and will always have her in our hearts.

Now, Jeff told us of your problem with Esther. He asked if we would take the baby until you are free to care for her. If we had known of this, he would not have had to ask, Nelson. All of us have prayed about this, and you must send the baby to us at once. If you cannot do so, one of us will come and get her. We do this because we love you and because we are all part of God's family.

This may be hard for you. You may think of it as pity. But we know that you and Irene would have done the same for us if we had been in such a situation.

It will be our joy to have Esther until you can care for her.

Your friends,
Daniel and Mary Carter

Jeff's father put the letter back into his pocket and said huskily, "I think God must have led you to write that letter, son."

"Are we going to do it, Pa? Let the Carters take care of Esther?"

"Yes. I'm convinced that it's of God. And you will have to take her to them, Jeff."

"Me!"

"Yes. You'll have to learn to fix her food. That's the most difficult thing. Dr. Bowden will help you with that." He spoke of the difficulties of the trip, then said, "It's a big responsibility, Jeff. Will you do it?"

Jeff nodded. "It was the last thing Ma asked, and I promised I'd take care of my sister."

"Good boy! We'll start getting ready for your trip right away." His father suddenly leaned over and grasped Jeff's shoulder. "I'm proud of you, Jeff —and your mother would be too!"

5
Boy with a Baby

Son, I wish I could do this for you or at least go with you." Nelson Majors stood looking at Jeff. His hazel eyes were troubled. Jeff and his father were standing on the platform of the Richmond railway terminal, waiting for the train to pull out.

"Don't worry, Pa," Jeff said quickly. "I'll be all right." He knew his father was worried about the trip, and Jeff wanted to assure him that things would go well. He gave the bundle in his arms a quick toss and said, "Esther and me—why, we'll make this trip just fine!"

The efforts that had been made to get this far had exhausted Jeff—although he did not say so to his father. He had spent a great deal of time with several mothers, all married to men in the regiment and all full of advice on how to take care of newborn infants. Some of them, he knew, were against what he was about to do.

"Why, you haven't got any sense at all!" one tall raw-boned woman had said. "The very thought of it—taking a brand new baby halfway across the state, and you no more than a baby yourself! Humph!"

Others had been more genial and encouraging.

Jeff had absorbed all the advice that his head would hold. But he had said to Tom, "I'd rather go into battle than make this trip! But don't tell Pa," he'd added quickly. "Esther and me—we'll make it all right."

The wood-burning engine uttered a shrill blast, and Jeff glanced over quickly at the plume of steam. "I guess we better get on the train, Pa," he said. "It looks like it's about ready to pull out."

"All right, son." The lieutenant looked at Jeff and said, "I'm very proud of you, you know." He gave the boy a tight hug, then pulled the blanket back from Esther's tiny face and studied it for a moment. Quickly he bent over and kissed the baby's red cheek. "I'll help you get your stuff on, Jeff."

The conductor looked carefully at the two as Jeff started to get on, followed by his father. "Guess your missus is coming?"

Nelson Majors paused with his foot on the step and shook his head. "No, I lost my companion. Be obliged to you if you'd keep an eye on my boy and the new baby there."

Sympathy rose in the blue eyes of the tall conductor. "Why sure, Lieutenant. You don't worry about a thing. I'll see that they get the best care the Alexandria and Orange Railroad's got."

They hurried into the car, and Jeff took a seat.

His father put down the large box he'd been carrying on the seat across from him. "Got to go," he said. "Son, get back as soon as you can." He clapped the boy on the shoulder, and then he was gone.

Jeff felt lonesome as his father left and the train pulled out. Through the window he saw his father diminish in the distance—and felt even worse. He had never gone on a long journey by himself before, and despite the front he had put up before his father and his brother, he was a little apprehensive.

The train picked up speed, and the outbuildings of Richmond began to flash by. The train gave two shrill blasts as it crossed a bridge. Soon the clatter of the wheels made a regular rhythm.

As the train sped along, Jeff thought, *Well, I'm on my way. I wish I was there already!*

The scenery rushed by. Jeff rocked back and forth as the train made several sharp turns. The roadbed was uneven, and he was jolted roughly as they passed over the junctions. Beside the track he saw section hands leaning on their shovels. They waved as the train passed, their teeth white against their black faces.

An hour later, Esther woke up suddenly. As always, she uttered a cry almost as loud as the shrill whistle of the steam engine itself.

Jeff felt his face redden, as everybody in the car looked around. He was aware that there were only two women present. Mostly the car was filled with soldiers, primarily privates but also some officers and several non-coms.

"All right, all right, baby sister," he whispered. "Don't blow the top of this car off!" Quickly he changed her diaper. That job had been very embarrassing for him at first, but the ladies had taught him how to do the chore easily, and it went well.

Next was the feeding, and he was less certain about this. The plan had been to try to find fresh milk along the way. To begin the trip, he carried a large bottleful, and he transferred some of this to a smaller bottle with a nipple made of cloth. He tried this for a while, but Esther grew red in the face and uttered another piercing scream, so Jeff went to plan number two.

He fished a small dish out of his box and mixed some milk with cereal that the ladies had concocted. Quickly he put Esther in his left arm, took a spoon, and put a portion of it in her mouth. *You look like a baby bird*, he thought.

She gulped eagerly, and Jeff sighed with relief as the shrill voice dwindled to a series of noisy grunts.

"Well, you're having quite a time, aren't you, son?"

Jeff looked up, startled, and saw the conductor standing by him. He was a tall man with red hair.

"Yes, sir . . . well . . . no, sir, I mean." Jeff was a little embarrassed, for everyone in the car was listening to the conversation.

"Your pa told me about losing your ma," the conductor said. "Right sorry to hear that." When Jeff mumbled his thanks, the man said, "That's a fine baby there. Boy or girl?"

"Girl—her name's Esther." Jeff reached in his pocket, got out his ticket, and handed it to the conductor.

"Kentucky, eh? Well, you got people there, I guess."

Jeff considered that quickly and thought it would be easier to agree.

"Yes, sir. I'll be coming back to Richmond, sir, after I get Esther to our people there."

The conductor sat down across from him and chatted for a while as the train rattled through the countryside. At last he said, "Well, Jeff, you let me know if you need anything. We've got plenty of blankets back in the caboose. What do you say I bring some and we make a bed for this young lady so she can sleep good?"

"Oh, that'd be fine."

Soon the conductor returned with several blankets. He helped fussily as they made a bed for Esther on the seat. By the time that was done, several people had come over to offer their advice, especially the two women.

"You'd better let me burp that child," one of them said.

Jeff said quickly, "Thank you, ma'am. I appreciate it." He surrendered Esther, and the woman competently carried out that chore and then rocked her back and forth. "Reminds me of one of my own," she said with a thoughtful look in her eye. She was an older lady with gray hair and was poorly dressed. She held the baby gently, then looked at her face and said, "What a beautiful child—and a beautiful name too!" She helped Jeff get Esther settled and then went back to her seat.

All that day, Jeff discovered he need not have worried about taking care of Esther. Everyone on the train seemed anxious to help, even a rough, burly sergeant, who informed them that he was in Jackson's brigade.

That night, as the train moved on through the darkness, the sergeant, whose name was Simms, sat down beside him, and the two talked for a long time. "I got two babies like that one. Little bit older," he said. "Don't guess I'll see 'em till this here war's over."

"Where do you live, Sergeant Simms?"

"Alabama, just outside of Montgomery. Got a farm out there, a wife, and two kids. All settled down and ready to start raising my family when this blamed war blew up."

"Maybe it'll be over soon," Jeff said. "That's what a lot of people say."

Sergeant Simms peered at Esther's face, which was squeezed up very tightly. "That's a sweet child," he said. It sounded strange coming from such a rough-looking man, but Jeff saw that despite his rough appearance he loved children.

The next day and the following night, Jeff talked almost constantly to people on the train. Some got on. Some got off, and all of these came to bid him and Esther good-bye.

Finally, Sergeant Simms came and put out his large, hard hand and gave Jeff a good handshake. "Been pleased to meet you, Jeff, you and Esther there. When you get back to your father's brigade, you might find me close by. Alabama won't be too far away from wherever he is with the army in northern Virginia." He reached over and touched Esther's cheek with a large forefinger and smiled when she made a bubble with her round lips. "You take care of this sweet thing, you hear?"

"Yes, sir, I will."

Then the sergeant got off, turned, and gave Jeff a hearty wave. And the train pulled out.

Jeff thought of the sergeant for a long time as the train rattled along. *I sure hope nothing happens to Sergeant Simms.* It somehow made the war seem more real to know that the sergeant might get killed —and that his wife, Matilda, and his son, Jake, and his daughter, Eileen, might be a widow and orphans.

* * *

52

When Jeff got off the train at Pineville, he was greeted at once by the station agent, Lem Farley. "Why, Jeff Majors, what in the world . . ."

"Hello, Lem," Jeff said. He grinned at the surprise of the small man and said, "This is my sister, Esther. You haven't met her."

For the next five minutes, Jeff explained the situation to Farley and others who came around. Then he said, "I've got to get out to the Carter place."

A short, roly-poly farmer named Eddings said, "Why, Jeff, I'm headed home and have to go right by there. You and that youngun get right in my wagon."

Jeff was soon seated beside Mr. Eddings, who wanted to know all about what had happened. Jeff told him the story, and Eddings shook his head.

"We heard about your ma. Sure was sorry to hear it, Jeff. She was a mighty fine woman." He continued to speak of things that had happened since Jeff left. Two hours later he raised his hand and said, "There it is—and that looks like Leah, don't it?"

Jeff looked up quickly, and the first thing he saw was Leah flying out the door, her blonde hair stretched out almost straight behind her.

"Jeff! Jeff!" she called.

When the wagon stopped and he got down, he found himself surrounded by the Carters. All but Royal seemed to be there. The women were determined to hug him and kiss him, which he protested but didn't really mind too much.

"You let me have that baby," Mrs. Carter demanded, snatching Esther from him. She pulled back the blanket, regarded the large, owlish eyes that looked up at her, and cried, "Isn't she the sweetest thing you ever saw? Look at this, Sarah—Leah."

The women and girls, including Morena, stood admiring the baby, and Mr. Carter came to stand beside Jeff. "Well, son," he said, giving him a firm handshake, "I'm sorry about your ma—but I'm right glad that we've got a chance to be of some help to you."

"Shoot, Mr. Carter"—Jeff shook his head—"Me and Pa and Tom didn't know what to do." He looked at the small man and said, tentatively, "Are you sure it won't be too much—"

"Too much! Why, boy, look at those women! They'll have the time of their life. They'll just make a doll out of that youngun!"

And that was about the way it went. Jeff was lucky to catch even a glimpse of Esther the rest of the day, because either Mrs. Carter or one of her daughters was holding her.

"That youngun's feet won't never touch the ground, I don't think," Leah's father said with a twinkle. "Now you come on with me and let them take care of that youngun."

It was a good time for Jeff. He had been tense, unsure of himself, unsure of what he would do or what was the right thing to do. But when he went to sleep that night, it was with a great sense of relief.

He said aloud, "Thank You, Lord, for getting us here and taking care of us, and just keep on taking care of Esther, will You please—and thank You so much for people like the Carters!"

* * *

54

"You remember this tree, Jeff? This is where we found the Baltimore oriole's egg."

Jeff looked up at the towering hickory, now covered with tiny green leaves, slightly gold at the tip. He nodded and smiled at the memory. "Why, sure I do! It was way up at the top there, and I nearly broke my neck trying to get it for you."

Leah laughed and reached out to pull his hair. "I remember that. Scared me to death. I thought you *were* going to break your neck."

"Ow!" Jeff caught her hand. "Will you stop pulling my hair? You always did do that—and you know how I hate it!"

Leah started to pull her hand back, but he held it firmly.

"I guess I ought to be more ladylike," she said suddenly. "After all, I'm thirteen years old now."

"You're real old, all right." Jeff grinned at her. His hair was black as a crow's wing when the sun hit it, and his eyes almost as black. He stood looking down at her and holding her hand. "You sure do have small arms. Why, my fingers almost go around your arm twice. You're going to have to get your ma to feed you more so you can get some fat on your bones."

Leah pulled her hand away, her eyes flashing. "I don't want to be fat," she snapped.

As a matter of fact, Jeff had noticed that even the short time he had been away—or perhaps because of the fact that he had been away—Leah seemed to have grown up. She was not much taller, but she had filled out. He didn't comment on this except to say, "Well, I don't reckon you have to worry about that."

"Come on, let's go down to the stream. Maybe we'll see old Napoleon down there, and we can catch him."

"All right."

The two ambled along until they reached the bridge. They leaned against the rail and looked over, and Jeff said, "Do you remember the last time we were here? We went home and heard about the war starting."

"I remember. I wish it would have never happened—that old war." Suddenly she turned to him. "Jeff, why don't you stay here with us? Pa needs help on the farm, and it would be a good place for you."

Jeff shook his head. "No, I'm going back." He hesitated and said, "I haven't told my pa about this, but I'm going in the army."

"In the army?" Leah looked at him with shock in her eyes. "Why, you can't go in the army—you're only fourteen years old."

"I can go in as a drummer boy," Jeff said stubbornly. "And I'm going to. It won't be long before this war will be over, and I want to see some of it." Leah stared at him, and then she smiled. She had always had an attractive smile. She announced, "I'm going in the army too."

Jeff's jaw dropped open.

He must have looked comical, for she laughed out loud. Her laughter had a trilling sound, very attractive to him, and she said, "Well, not really going in the army. I'm going to be a vivandière."

"You're going to be a what?"

"A vee-von-dee-ay." Leah pronounced the word slowly. "That's just a fancy French word. It means a young woman who goes and sells things to the soldiers. You see, Jeff, Pa's going to be a sutler, and I'm going with him—mostly to take care of him. He's not too strong, you know. So we'll be following the army wherever it goes, selling the soldiers needles and thread and passing out Bibles and tracts to them all."

They walked on deep into the woods, enjoying the breeze and the sun. Finally Jeff looked around the green walls of the forest and said, "I don't know when I'll ever get back here, Leah. And when I do, you'll be gone."

"Let's don't say that!" She shook her head violently. "Let's think it will be over soon, and your pa and Tom will be back, and you'll be here, and I'll be here."

"I wish it was now." He told her about Sergeant Simms. "What if something happened to him? There he'd have a widow and two babies left."

"I know," Leah said. "I worry about Royal. Something could happen to him. I worry about your pa and Tom too."

A thoughtful look came into her eyes. "Sarah worries about Tom all the time. Do you suppose," she asked, "that when the war's over they'll get married?"

"I don't know."

"If they did, that'd make us cousins, wouldn't it? Or something like that?"

Jeff grinned. "You don't know much about how to get to be cousins, do you? I guess we'd be in-laws of some kind, though."

They came out of the woods and approached the house.

Jeff said abruptly, "I'll be leaving tomorrow, so I'll just say my thanks here to you. I've already said it a hundred times to your ma and pa. You sure got some fine folks, Leah."

Leah reached out and touched his arm. "It makes me sad to think about separating. I like for people to be close when they are friends." She stopped briefly, then said, "You know you're my best friend, Jeff. You always have been."

Jeff put his hand out and took hers. He shook it firmly and said, "Well, shoot! You're my best friend too, Leah . . ."

He would have said more, but her mother came out and called, "Hurry up, supper's almost ready."

Jeff left the next morning, and the thing he remembered most clearly about his departure was Esther's crying when he walked out the door—and the tears in Leah's eyes.

6

The Sutlers

Leah looked over the pile of supplies stacked high in the wagon. "Pa, it looks like this is about all we can carry."

Her father had been trying to force a small package full of needles into a crevice. He turned and shrugged his shoulders, and a smile was on his thin lips. "I guess you're right, Leah. Don't even have room left for this last package." He shoved it into his pocket instead. "Well, let's go say good-bye to the folks. We need to be on our way."

They climbed out of the wagon and returned to the house where the family was gathered around the breakfast table.

Leah's mother shook her head and put her hands on her hips. "I hope you two don't think you're going to get away without eating breakfast! Sit down now. You'll get at least one good meal. No telling when you'll get another one."

"Now, Ma, that's real fine," her husband said. He put his arm around her and gave her a hug. "I know Leah and I will miss your good cooking. There's not another cook like you."

Then the family enjoyed a breakfast of battered eggs, pork sausage, large biscuits, grits, and plenty of fresh milk and coffee to wash it all down.

"I guess we got everything loaded," Mr. Carter said as he shoved a bit of biscuit in his mouth and chewed on it thoughtfully. "If we got any more in that wagon, I don't think Buck and Jake could pull the load. They're good mules, but there's a limit even to a mule."

His wife looked up and said sharply, "There's a limit on men too. Now, Dan, I want you to promise me, if you can't make it, come on home." She cut off his words and shook her head firmly. "Leah, you make him mind, you hear? Bring him home if he gets to feeling too bad."

"We'll make it fine, Mama. I'll take care of him. You know I will."

After breakfast they all gathered outside, and for just one moment Dan bowed his head. They held hands as he said a quick prayer. He ended by saying, "And, O God, take care of our people—Mary and the children here while Leah and I go to minister to the soldiers. We trust You for this in Jesus' name. Amen."

A murmur of amens went up, and Leah went at once to hug Morena, who smiled up at her and gave her a quick kiss on the cheek. "You be sweet, Morena," Leah whispered. Then she went to Sarah and her mother and gave them both hugs.

Finally Leah and her father were in the wagon, and they rolled out of the yard, waving at those left behind.

When they were out of sight of the house, Leah said, "You know, Pa, I feel a little funny, don't you?"

He shoved his straw hat back on his head and scratched the bridge of his nose. "I guess so, Pet. But we know this is the Lord's work, so we'll be all right. Do you think we got everything?"

Leah pulled a list out of her pocket. She was wearing a brown-and-pink, oversized, checked gingham dress today, and a bonnet over her curls. She studied the list and named off some of the items. "Let's see. We got pens, ink, razors, lots of candy, food—mostly sweet things—and lots of tracts and Bibles." She gave her father a warm smile. "Oh, Pa, this is going to be so much fun."

He scratched his chin thoughtfully and gave her a cautious look. "Well," he murmured, "it's going to be a little more than a Sunday school picnic, I reckon."

They drove all day long, just pausing at noon for a quick meal. That night they made camp beside a small stream. Leah did the cooking after her father had built a fire, and afterward they sat around looking into the flame and talking about what was to come.

"I guess we'll be doing this a lot," Mr. Carter said, nodding sleepily. The trip had tired him, and his face was drawn. "We'll be moving right along with the soldiers, and that'll mean making camp every night just like we did tonight."

Leah was not deceived by his cheerful words. She had learned to recognize the signs of fatigue on his face, but she didn't mention this. Instead she stretched and yawned hugely, saying, "Oh, Pa, I'm so tired! Let's go to bed early tonight and sleep as late as we can."

"Why, if you're tired, I guess that's what we better do," he said, apparently fooled by her tactics.

She made her bed inside the wagon, using blankets and a goose-feather pillow. There was barely room for her to make it, so filled was the wagon with supplies. When she finally had put on her nightgown and pulled a light blanket over her, she said, "Good night, Pa."

61

From beneath the wagon, where her father had made his bed, came the sleepy answer. "Good night, daughter. You sleep well. Won't be long before we'll be seeing some of the soldiers." Silence ran over the camp, and finally he muttered, "I hope we get to see Royal. I sure do miss that boy."

Leah lay quietly, unable to sleep. She was not as tired as she had pretended, but she wanted her father to get a good night's rest. For a long time she lay there, listening to the gurgling of the creek as it ran over the stones and to the chirping of crickets as they punctuated the silence of the night.

Finally, she said her prayers, asking at the last, "Help me take care of Pa, Lord, and we'll be all right."

* * *

"Well, Leah, what do you think of Washington?"

They had entered the capital and were driving along the main thoroughfare, which was 160 feet wide and more than 4 miles long. To get there, Leah's father had driven through the center market—where gambling houses operated openly—and through Swampoodle and other slums.

They were traveling along the Old City Canal, a fetid bayou filled with floating dead cats and all kinds of garbage. It reeked with terrible odors. Cattle, sheep, swine, and geese scattered before the mules' hooves as they made their way along.

Now, as they approached the outskirts of the city, having gone all the way through it, Leah made a face at her father. "It stinks!" she exclaimed.

"Yes, it does," her father agreed. "I hope the camp will smell better." He looked back under the canvas of the heavily loaded wagon. "We'll have to get permission to set up. I just hope I don't have to pay too large a bribe."

"What's that?"

"Well, every sutler has to buy a license. But that's only the beginning. If what I hear is true, there'll be other palms to grease before we can do business."

"Why, Pa, that's terrible."

"Well, it's the way the world works, Leah." Her father shrugged. "If we want to help the soldiers, we'll just have to pay for the privilege."

By the time they reached the camp, the sun was high in the sky. A corporal asked to see their pass and then directed them. "You'll have to go to regimental headquarters to get your permit," he said.

As the two drove along, Leah was overwhelmed at the tremendous activity in the camp. Sergeants were yelling at their squads. Horses raced by carrying couriers, and caissons rumbled past—sometimes forcing their wagon off the narrow road. Somehow they found their way to a large tent having a narrow pennant waving over it.

"I guess that's it," her father said. "Come on along, and we'll get our permit."

Getting the permit proved to be a relatively complicated business. They had to work their way up to a clerk who was a corporal to the major of the regiment. They recognized the major at once.

"Why, Major Bates," Leah's father said, "I'm glad to see you here." When the major looked at him without recognition, he added, "I'm Dan Carter. My boy, Royal, is a member of your regiment. You enlisted him there in Pineville."

Major Bates nodded, as recognition came to his eyes. "Why, yes, I do remember. What are you doing here? Just come to see your boy?"

"Oh, no, Major Bates. We've come to join you as sutlers. Got my wagon waiting right outside, ready to go to work."

"Why, that's fine! We need good men like you, sir." He looked at Leah. "And who is this young lady?"

"That's my daughter, Leah. She takes care of me while I take care of the supplies."

Major Bates leaned back and stared at her. He stroked his chin thoughtfully and said, "Well, I'm afraid that'll make things more difficult."

"Why is that, Major?"

"You know how soldiers are." The major shrugged. "Some of them are pretty rough, and the profanity's fierce. I'd hate for this young lady to be subjected to it."

"That's all right, Major," Leah said at once. "My brother is here, and if the rest of the soldiers are like him, they won't offend me."

Bates laughed and slapped his thigh. "Well, I suppose that answers it then. Here—let me give you this permit." He scribbled his name on the sheet given him by the corporal, handed it to Dan Carter, and said, "I've heard a good report of your son. If I'm not mistaken, he's already been made a corporal. I suppose you'd like to see him?"

"Yes, we would, if it's not too much trouble."

"No trouble at all," the major said expansively. He turned to the corporal, who was sitting opposite at a desk. "Corporal, take Mr. Carter and his daughter over to Company A."

"Yes, sir."

64

The corporal rose at once and climbed onto the wagon seat. He was a heavy young man, and the seat was narrow, so he squeezed against Leah. He grinned at her and winked. "This wagon wasn't made for a big fellow like me, was it?" Then he directed her father down the crowded street.

It all seemed a maze to Leah. The tents were orderly enough, but the corporal directed them down several streets, and she became turned around.

"You'll get used to it," he said. He raised his arm and pointed. "Right over there is Company A. I'll just walk back. You can find your boy somewhere drilling, I guess."

"Thank you, Corporal." Mr. Carter reached in his pocket and pulled out a small New Testament and handed it to the surprised soldier. "Like for you to have this," he said. "Every man needs the Word of God, doesn't he?"

The corporal took it gingerly, looked at it, then nodded with a smile. "Thanks a lot. I'll sure read it." He stuck it in his pocket, turned, and walked away.

"Well, our first Bible given away, Pa." Leah smiled. "I hope he does read it."

"All we can do is sow the seed. But I've got the feeling that if we're faithful, God will use His Word mightily. Come on, let's go see if we can find your brother."

Thirty minutes later they were talking excitedly with Royal. They had found him drilling, but his sergeant, who had looked up and seen the visitors coming, shouted, "Squads, dismissed."

Royal shook his father's hand and gave Leah a hug, sweeping her off her feet. "Shucks, I didn't expect to see you here!" he exclaimed. His face was sunburned, and he seemed to have lost weight.

"How are you, boy?" his father asked quickly.

"Oh, I'm fine." Royal shrugged. "Soldiering isn't like I thought it would be, though."

"How's that?"

"Why, I guess I thought we'd be marching right off to fight the Rebels!" He grinned sheepishly. "But look at this." He held out a wooden gun and gave a half laugh. "You can't stop the Rebels with wooden guns, can you now?"

"Why'd they give you that?" Leah asked curiously.

"Because there's not enough real guns to supply the army. I guess we'll be getting them soon enough. Come on, let me see your wagon."

As he turned to go, Royal suddenly called to a young man standing watching them. "Hey, Tuck, come on. I want you to meet my family."

The young man who approached was no more than seventeen. He had light blue eyes and a shock of coal-colored hair and a liberal supply of freckles across his sunburned skin. "This is Tuck Givens. We came into the regiment together," Royal explained. "This is my father, and my sister, Leah."

"Pleased to meet you," Tuck mumbled. He shook Mr. Carter's hand and nodded bashfully toward Leah. "Royal's been telling me all about you."

"Well, come on, and I'll tell them all about you," Royal said. He winked at Leah. "You want to watch out for him, Leah. Givens is a lady-killer."

"Aw, shoot!" exclaimed Tuck, his face flushing. "Don't you believe a word of that." He glanced again at Leah. When he saw that she was laughing

66

at him, a grin spread across his wide lips. "This brother of yours, he's really something."

The four made their way to the wagon, and Tuck and Royal helped them find the park where the other sutlers had set up camp. There were six sutlers in all, and nothing would do but that the two young men would set up the tent that Leah and her father would share.

When they were through, Royal looked toward the wagon. "Pa, looks like you got your first customers already. Look at 'em—they're swarming like bees."

Indeed, a large group of soldiers had gathered around the wagon.

"Well, that's good. You come and help me, Royal—you can introduce me to some of your friends."

Leah moved to go with him, but Royal said, "Let me help Pa this time. Tuck, you show Leah around the camp." He winked again, saying, "You watch out for him, Leah. I've told you what a fellow he is with the girls."

When the two men left, Tuck bit his lip and said, "Well, Miss Carter, I'd be glad to show you the camp if you'd like to see it."

"Yes, I haven't ever seen anything like it. But you can call me Leah, if I can call you Tuck." She smiled at him, cocking her head to one side and making an attractive picture. "What a funny name! Is that your real name, Tuck?"

"Aw, no. Just a nickname. My real name is Robert—but Tuck is fine."

For the next hour the young soldier showed Leah as much of the camp as could be covered on foot. She was fascinated by the drill teams and by the large herd of cavalry horses. Then she was fortunate enough to witness a cavalry charge on a large, open field.

As they watched, Tuck said, "I sure wish I was in the cavalry! It beats walking. They walk us about ten to fifteen miles a day, it seems like."

"Why don't you join the cavalry then?"

"Oh, that's a pretty fancy outfit. I guess I'll just stick with the infantry." He hesitated. "Your brother, Royal, he's a fine fellow. I'd hate to leave him now. We've become good friends."

As the two walked back, Leah found herself wondering about the young men such as Tuck Givens. They had come from all over the North to form this army that was being put together, and she realized that this was only the beginning. The training and the drill would soon be over, and, sometime out in the future, young men like Tuck Givens would be dying. She didn't want to think of that, so she spoke cheerfully of other things as they returned to the wagon.

* * *

The army seemed in no hurry to pull out. Leah settled down, waiting every day for the call that would inform them the soldiers were leaving. But days went by that turned into weeks. May was approaching its end, and still the men did their daily drill. Almost every day, finely dressed ladies came out from the capital accompanied by their equally finely dressed husbands. The aristocracy of Washington came to watch the drills, and more than once some of them came by to talk to Leah and her father.

They were fascinated by the young girl, it seemed. One of them said severely, "I wouldn't let my daughter be around these soldiers. I'm surprised at you, sir!"

Dan smiled gently. "I discovered, ma'am, that virtue is the same in camp or out—that goodness endures no matter where it goes."

The woman sniffed, turned, and walked away.

Leah laughed out loud after she was gone. "You hurt her feelings, Pa."

"Well, maybe she's got something on her side. I can see how people would be worried." He gave Leah a look and said, "You have heard some rough talk, I guess?"

"Oh, sometimes the men forget, but mostly they've been real careful."

Her father laughed. "I can understand that—after Royal pounded the daylights out of that soldier who cussed in front of you. That was an object lesson, I guess you might call it."

Leah flushed as she remembered the incident. "I guess that had something to do with it—but they're mostly really nice boys. They're so young, Pa! It's hard to think about them going out and maybe dying."

His eyes were sober. "And they're dying right now in the hospital." He bit his lip. "I never thought young men would die from measles."

Before the Federal and Confederate armies had even met, disease swept both camps—diphtheria, diarrhea, and most of all measles. In some companies, more than half the soldiers were down, and some of them had actually died.

Leah frowned. "You know, I'm worried about Tuck. Those measles he got, they've drained all his strength."

"I know. I reckon we ought to go over and see him."

They made their way to the regimental hospital, and when they went down the aisles of beds, many of the soldiers spoke, for Leah and her father had visited before, leaving tracts and small gifts.

Leah felt sorry for them. They all looked so young. "I wish we could stop and talk to all of them, Pa."

"Maybe we can come back later."

Then they arrived at Tuck's cot and saw that it was empty. "Why, he was here yesterday." Leah blinked in surprise. A male nurse was passing, and she said, "Has Private Givens been dismissed?"

The nurse, a tall, thin man with a full beard, hesitated. He fumbled at the button on his uniform. "No, miss." He hesitated again. "Are you his family?"

"Oh, no, we're just friends of his." A premonition came to Leah, and she asked in alarm, "He *is* all right, isn't he?"

The nurse shook his head. "He took real bad, miss, last night. His fever shot up—and there wasn't nothing we could do for him."

Leah and her father stared at the man in horror.

"You don't mean," Mr. Carter whispered, "that he died?"

"I'm afraid so, sir. Too bad! Too bad!" The nurse shook his head. "He was a fine young man. All the men loved him in here." Sadness came into his eyes, and he stroked his beard. "I never get used to it," he murmured. "All these young men come to fight for their country, and they die of measles! Too bad. Too bad!"

Leah walked away quickly, tears blinding her eyes. She was aware that her father was beside her, and when they were outside she turned to him and whispered, "Oh, Pa, how awful! He was such a fine young man . . . and to die like that . . . away from home, among strangers . . ."

"But he was a Christian," Mr. Carter said. "We know that much, so we can be glad he's gone to be with Jesus—as sad as it is to lose him."

He looked over the hospital tent and murmured, "How many more will have to die before this war is over?"

7
Mr. Lincoln

Leah had great difficulty getting over the death
of Tuck Givens. As a matter of fact, she never did
get over it—nor did she ever become accustomed
to the deaths that occurred daily among the troops.

"I don't think I can stand it, Pa!" she moaned
one day. "If it's this bad before they go to fight,
what will it be like afterwards?"

Washington had filled itself with young men
from all over the country. The capital park had become a drill ground, and soldiers stretched on the
grass in the shade to watch the activities of other
regiments.

The men of the First Rhode Island spread their
bunks beside the patent office. They were dressed
in simple coarse uniforms—gray pants, dark blue
flannel shirts, and army hats turned up at the side.
Across their shoulders they slung their scarlet blanket rolls.

Daily the troops poured in, until finally Mr.
Carter exclaimed one day, "There's only so many
cats you can put in a sack! I don't know how many
more soldiers they think they can stuff into this
town."

But the Washington populace greeted the new-
comers with glee. There had been rumors that the
South was mounting an invasion, and Congress and
the people welcomed the soldiers. A high board
fence had to be built at the depot to protect the

troops from the cheering crowds. Every day the population turned out to see them parade onto the avenue. From New Jersey came 3,200 men, the largest group that Washington had ever seen in line. The well-equipped regiments received their baggage and were sent to make camp on the hills around the city.

By the middle of May, vast loads of freight were coming to Washington by rail and by the Potomac. The navy yard was filled with steamers, schooners, and tugs carrying thousands of blankets and tons of coal, hard bread, and groceries. A herd of cattle ordered to provide fresh beef for the soldiers was put on the grounds of the Washington Monument. Many of them fell into the canal. It took a day and a half to drive them back to the shore, and six fine beefs were drowned.

Daily they flowed in, and a gaily dressed and carefree crowd strolled through the grounds to the tune of "Yankee Doodle," "Upidee," "The Girl I Left Behind Me," and "Columbia, the Gem of the Ocean." Saturday afternoon Marine band concerts went on regularly, and the president hoisted the big new flag contributed by the clerks of the Interior Department.

One regiment of New Yorkers attracted more attention than others—the Seventh Infantry. A young man named Elmer Ellsworth had recruited a regiment from the volunteer fire departments. A gang of roughs dressed in gray, scarlet, and blue Zouave costumes were armed with rifles and huge bowie knives and encumbered with handsome presentation flags.

Heavy-shouldered, hard-faced, spoiling for a fight, the fiery Zouaves tumbled off the cars asking for Jeff Davis and growling over the fact that they had not gotten into battle yet. As they marched up the avenue, Ellsworth took the cheers of the gathering crowds. His Zouaves were ready for battle, he declared.

The fiery Zouaves had little respect for anything. In their gaudy, fancy dress they swung themselves down ropes from the cornice of the Rotunda and hung like monkeys from the edge of the Capitol dome. They had great respect for their little colonel but were as wild as wharf rats. One day some seized a wandering pig, cut its throat, and ate it. They bought new shoes at a fashionable bootmaker's and directed the bill be sent to Old Abe— President Lincoln. Dinners and suppers, cigars and transportation, were charged to Jeff Davis.

So Washington's prayers for soldiers were answered. The country town had been turned into a great confused garrison, and the entertaining novelty soon began to pall. Quiet residential neighborhoods were in an uproar. Soldiers drilled and bugled and drummed all over the place. Irresponsible as children, they fired their weapons in any direction—in the streets and even in houses.

Leah and her father could not keep enough supplies. The soldiers quickly bought them out, which meant they had to make trips into the city to get more and more supplies for their wagon. They gave away many tracts and Bibles, and almost every night there was a religious service somewhere in the vicinity of the camp.

Royal and his friend Jay Walters, who had enlisted with him in Pineville, spent a great deal of time with Dan Carter and Leah.

Another young fellow had joined Royal, whose name was Ira Pickens. Pickens was a tall, lean youth with a head of bushy black hair. He was plain almost to the point of ugliness but spent a great deal of time boasting about his sweetheart back home in Rhode Island—Rosie.

One day Ira approached Leah with a request. She could see he was nervous and tried to put him at ease. "What is it, Ira? Do you need some supplies?"

"Uh . . . no . . . I don't need nothing out of your wagon, but—" He broke off and stared at the ground. He was obviously embarrassed and could not go on.

Leah had grown accustomed to the bashfulness of many of the soldiers and asked at once, "What is it, Ira? You know I'll help you if I can."

Ira lifted his eyes and said, "Well, the thing is, I can't write."

This did not come as a surprise to Leah. Many of the young men could not, especially those from backwoods districts.

Pickens bit his lip. "You know I had to leave my gal Rosie when I jined the army, and I'm afraid some of them fellows that didn't jine up are giving her the rush. Since I can't go back and whup 'em, I guess the onliest thing I can do is write her letters."

"Oh, why I'd be glad to write her for you. Just a minute." Leah bustled around, got pen and paper and ink, and sat herself down at the small table just outside their tent. "You just say what you want, and I'll put it down for you, Ira."

Ira slumped down on a nail keg and began to pull at his long bushy hair. Strain came into his eyes as he tried to find the words. Finally he said, haltingly, "Dear Rosie. I am fine. How are you?"

75

He stopped and looked over, saying, "I can't think of nothing to say."

"Why, of course you can," Leah encouraged. "Just tell her what you've been doing."

Pickens brightened, and for the next ten minutes he dictated slowly the account of his activities. Then he said, "Yours truly, Ira Pickens."

Leah looked up and smiled. "Why, you can't end a letter like that, Ira!"

"Why not?" Pickens was truly surprised.

"This is a letter you might write to your father or your sister," she protested. She cocked her head to one side and bit the end of her pen. "Rosie's your sweetheart, isn't she?"

"Well, I reckon so."

"Well, then, you've got to say more than 'I went to drill this morning.' You've got to say something sweet."

"Sweet? Like what?"

Leah tried to hide the smile that came to her lips. It struck her as amusing that the tall soldier had no more idea of how to write a love letter than he had of writing an encyclopedia.

"Why, tell her that you miss her. Tell her how pretty she looked the last time you saw her, and tell her that you love her. Ask her to be faithful to you."

Ira Pickens perked up. "Yeah," he said brightly. "Say all that, Leah."

Leah laughed. "Why, I can't put down what I say," she protested. "Rosie wants to hear what *you* have to say."

Pickens slumped down again and shook his head dolefully. "Aw, I ain't never had no practice much talking like that!"

76

Leah thought for a moment. "Why don't you write her a poem?"

"A poem?" Pickens stared at her blankly. If she had asked him to jump over the sun he could not have been more surprised. "Why, Miss Leah, that's crazy. If I can't write no letter, how'm I going to write a poem?"

"Well," Leah confessed, "I guess that is a bit much. But you've got to put a little romance in your letter, Ira. Young ladies expect it."

"Do you get letters from your sweetheart, Miss Leah?"

Leah blushed, "Why—"

"I expect you do got a suitor, ain't you?"

"Why, I'm only thirteen years old!" Leah said. "I'm too young for things like that."

But Pickens must have seen her blush, and he was a sharp young man despite his backwardness. He studied her carefully, then grinned. "I bet you have got some young fella that you like, ain't you, now?"

Leah tried to deny it, but when he persisted she said, "Well, I do have a friend. We grew up together. His name is Jeff, and we write. I do think a lot about him."

"Whereabouts is he?"

Leah's face grew sad. She shook her head and said, "He's in Virginia. His father's in the Confederate army."

"Aw, that's too bad, Miss Leah," Ira said. "It's terrible, ain't it—the way this war's done tore people up." He sat there, a lank shape, his homely face in repose. Finally he said, "Well, you write that letter for me, and I'll make my mark at the end. Rosie knows I can't write, but she'll know my mark."

77

Several times during the next few weeks, Ira came to dictate other letters to Rosie. He took considerable jesting from his fellow soldiers, but he never seemed to grow angry. "That's all right," he said to Leah. "Let 'em make fun of me. But with letters like you've been writing, why, them other fellas back home ain't got a chance."

"Why don't you let me teach you how to write, Ira?" Leah asked. "You're smart enough—it wouldn't take you any time to learn."

Ira shook his head. "Naw, I reckon not. I got me a good letter-writer already, and I'm thinking this shooting will be over before I have time to learn anything as complicated as writing. Naw, you just keep writing to Rosie for me."

* * *

It was on a fine afternoon the last of May that Mr. Lincoln came down to inspect the army. All of the companies were driven by their sergeants into their best appearance. Buckles were polished, uniforms had to be neatly pressed and beards trimmed.

And on the afternoon President Lincoln came, Leah and her father were close enough to see him where he stood in his box.

"My, he's tall, isn't he?" Leah said. She studied his face. "And he doesn't look at all like a gorilla—not like those Southern newspapers call him."

"No," her father agreed, "he's got a kind look on his face, hasn't he? I think he's just the man we need for our president."

For the next two hours the two stood and watched the parade.

First the infantry strutted by. Company after company divided into brigades, their buttons sparkling in the sun, as—bayonets fixed and gleaming—they marched past the president's box.

Then the ground rumbled as teams drew the caissons and cannons by—row after row of them, one man seated on a horse, the other seated on the caisson. After this came a thundering charge by the cavalry, all dressed in blue, their sabers drawn, flashing in the sun.

Next was a demonstration of artillery fire so that the ground seemed to shake with the sound of the explosions.

Finally, it was over. Leah and her father went back at once to their wagon, knowing they would be besieged by the soldiers on such an occasion as this. They had laid in a large store of good things to eat, and, as the soldiers crowded around, Mr. Carter murmured, "I wish we could just give this away to these fine young men."

"If we did that," Leah said practically, "we wouldn't be able to buy any more to pass out to the others." She was aware that her father was making very little money. He couldn't bear to see a young soldier who had no money go away empty-handed.

They worked hard for an hour, and finally the crowd thinned out. All of a sudden someone said, "Look, there he is—Mr. Lincoln!"

Leah looked up in surprise. The president, accompanied by several government leaders and a group of officers, was making his way down through the troops. Every once in a while, President Lincoln would stop and talk to a lowly private and shake his hand.

"Pa, he's coming this way!" Leah whispered with excitement. "I'd give anything just to shake his hand."

79

Then Abraham Lincoln paused right in front of their wagon. His warm brown eyes fell on her, and he advanced at once. He seemed very tall as he looked down at Leah.

"Well, young lady, I'm glad to see you here serving our fine soldiers."

"Yes, sir." She stumbled, barely able to speak for excitement. "My father and I, we came to do all we could for the Union."

"And what might your name be?" the president inquired.

"I'm Leah Carter, and this is my father, Daniel," Leah answered quickly. "And my brother, Royal, is in A Company."

"So the whole family has come to help the Union?" The president smiled. He did have a homely face, but there was a kindness and a warmth in it that seemed to shed light as he looked around. He shook hands with her father, saying, "You are to be congratulated, sir, on your efforts."

Daniel Carter cleared his throat and nodded. "Mr. President, I pray for you every day of my life. I know the heavy burden that you're under, and I pray that God will give you strength to bear it."

Lincoln's eyes opened wide, and he grew sober. "I thank you, sir, and I encourage you to continue to do so. Without the help of the Almighty there is no way that I could carry this burden, but with His help we cannot fail."

A murmur of appreciation ran around, and Leah suddenly put out her hand. "Mr. Lincoln," she said, "can I shake your hand?"

At once her hand was enclosed in the president's. It was so large that hers seemed lost, but he held it gently. "Well, I never refuse a chance to shake hands with an attractive young woman," Lincoln said with a smile. "Where are you from, Miss Leah?"

"From Kentucky, sir."

"Ah, yes, Kentucky." Lincoln shook his head sadly. "One of our border states, neither Confederate nor Federal. You have great problems there."

"Yes, sir. Many of our friends went to be with the South."

"Yes, I too have fine friends in the South," Lincoln said at once. "We must pray that one day soon we will all be united again."

Leah looked up and asked before she thought, "Will we win, Mr. President?"

Lincoln stared at her for a long moment, then whispered, "Yes, Miss Leah, I must believe that the Almighty will bring this country back under one flag again." He studied her. "You worry about your friends and perhaps relatives in the South?"

"Yes, sir, I do."

Lincoln nodded. "A sad thing." He hesitated and then put his hand out again. When he had hers in his, he said, "I thank you on the part of your government for what you're doing to help our brave boys. If you ever need help that I can give, I hope you will come and ask for it."

And then he was gone.

Leah's hand seemed warm after the pressure of his. As she watched the president walk away, surrounded by the officers and statesmen, she thought suddenly of Jeff so far away in the South. Sadness came over her, but she thought of the president's words—"The Almighty will bring this country back under one flag again," and she whispered,

"Pa, he's right, isn't he? One day this will all be over."

Dan Carter put his hand on her shoulder and whispered, "Yes, daughter, one day it'll all be over, and we'll be one people again."

8

A New Recruit

As Jeff stepped down off the train, he discovered that war fever had come to Richmond. A host of young men had flocked to the city to enlist, and he soon learned that their greatest fear was that the big battle would be over before they could become a part of it. As he pressed his way through the streets, the people behaved as though they were infected. They rushed from rally to rally, faces flushed, shouting war slogans.

"I guess I better go find Pa," he murmured and managed to make his way through the crowds. He noticed that the volunteer companies that were seeking to enlist new members had rather awe-inspiring names, such as Baker Fire-eaters, Southern Avengers, Bartol Yankee Killers, Cherokee Lincoln Killers, and Hornet's Nest Riflemen.

I hope they're as rough as their names, he thought with a smile.

He paused beside a platform where a battle flag made by the ladies of Richmond was to be presented. This company had the rather ferocious name of Southern Yankee Killers. Jeff watched as the volunteers stood in ranks, their eyes fixed on the speakers, who gave them a flowery tribute. Then the color sergeant advanced with his corporals to receive the flag, rising to the occasion with an impressive response:

"Ladies, with high beating hearts and pulses throbbing with emotion, we receive from your hands this beautiful flag, the proud emblem of our young republic. To those who will return from the field of battle bearing this flag—though it may be tattered and torn—in triumph, this incident will always prove a cheering recollection. And to him whose fate it may be to die a soldier's death, this moment brought before his fading view will recall your kind and sympathetic words. He will bless you as his spirit takes its aerial flight . . ."

Jeff stayed long enough to hear the speech and several others much like it. Finally the oratory stopped long enough for the soldiers to receive liberal offerings of cake, cookies, punch, and coffee from the young ladies, all of whom were adorned in their best dresses.

Being half starved from his long trip, Jeff edged over to one of the tables and managed to fill up on some of the sweets and the lemonade.

Finally, he left the heart of the city and made his way to the house his father had rented. When he got there, however, he was surprised to find six or seven small children ranging from a baby of no more than a year to a pugnacious boy of seven or eight.

He stopped abruptly, wondering if he had the right house, then shrugged and walked to the door. As he stepped inside, he was accosted at once by a very large woman, who demanded, "What are you doing in my house?"

Jeff blinked with surprise and then swallowed. "Why I . . . I live here."

The woman stared, and then her features softened. "Oh, then you'd be Lieutenant Majors's son, I'm thinking."

84

"Yes, I'm Jeff Majors." Jeff looked around and saw that the room was filled with items he had never seen before.

The woman, seeing his glance, said, "My name is Mrs. Taylor. My husband is a sergeant in your father's company. We had no place else to go, so Lieutenant Majors said we could stay here."

"Oh," Jeff said lamely and then added, "I guess you'll be here for quite a while."

Mrs. Taylor shrugged. "As long as the army's here. And then when they go off, I'll have to wait." She tucked a strand of hair back. "Don't worry— we'll fix a place for you somewhere."

Jeff at once said, "Don't bother, Mrs. Taylor. I'm going to see my father now. I just want to get some of my things."

"Well, we packed them in a box. But you won't find anyplace else to stay," she said abruptly. "Richmond's packed like a grape in its skin! No more room anywhere."

Jeff found a change of clothes, but it was so crowded in the room with several children staring at him that he said, "I'll change later. Thank you, Mrs. Taylor."

Leaving the house, he began his walk to camp. As he walked he thought, *I can't stay in that place. Why, I'd go crazy with all those kids!*

He reached the camp and, having walked all the way, was rather tired. At once he went to Company A and found his father sitting in the tent he used for an office.

"Jeff—you're back!" Nelson Majors leaped to his feet and moved over at once to call out the door, "Corporal Majors—come here."

Tom glanced up from where he was drilling a squad across the field and came running, once he saw Jeff. "Step into my office," their father said.

When the boys were inside, he shut the tent flap and grinned. "Can't let them see this." He stepped forward and gave Jeff a hug.

Tom did the same. "When did you get back?"

"This morning, about two hours ago." Jeff put his clothes down on the cot. "Looks like the house has been taken over, Pa."

"Yes, I had to let Mrs. Taylor stay there. Sergeant Taylor's a good man and didn't have anywhere to put his family. But they'll make room for you, I'm sure."

Jeff said nothing, for he wanted to speak to his father alone.

Tom said with a grin, "Tell us all about your trip. Some luck getting out of all this work and drill to go on a nice vacation!"

"It wasn't a vacation," Jeff said indignantly. "If you think it's fun taking a baby on a train ride across the country—"

"Oh, don't pay any attention to Tom," their father said. "Now, tell us about everything. How is Esther? How are the Carters?"

The three sat down, and for half an hour Jeff brought them up on the news of their former neighbors. He ended by saying, "We did the right thing to take Esther there, Pa. The Carters were tickled to death to have her. Why, Mrs. Carter acted like it was her own baby!"

Lieutenant Majors ran his hand through his black hair, a look of relief on his face. "I can't tell you how glad I am to hear that, Jeff. I don't know what we'd have done if it hadn't been for those good people."

"What about Leah?" Tom asked suddenly. "Did you get a good-bye kiss from her?"

Jeff flushed and snapped, "No, but it's none of your business what I got, Tom!"

Tom laughed. "I don't believe a word of that. That young lady's growing up in a hurry."

"Well, I have something for you. A letter from another young lady," Jeff said. "But since you're so cocky, I just won't give it to you."

"From Sarah?" At once Tom straightened up. "Give it here."

"Nope. If you treat me right, I'll—ow!"

Tom leaped across the tent and grabbed Jeff, throwing him to the ground. He held him there, squirming and protesting, as he went through his pockets. Finally Tom said, "Where is it, you varmint? I'll have it now!"

"Let him up, Tom," their father said. "It's against the rules for two members of this company to get into a fight." He helped Jeff to his feet. "Now, don't pay any attention to Tom. He means well—he just thinks he's funny."

Jeff gave Tom a baleful look and reached into his inner pocket. "Here's a letter for you, Pa, from Mr. Carter, and I think one from his wife in the same envelope." As his father took the envelope and opened it eagerly, Jeff handed the other letter he had extracted to Tom, saying, "There's your old letter, but you don't deserve it!"

Tom grinned. "Thanks, Jeff. I'll make it right with you." He ripped open the envelope and began to read.

Jeff watched his face. As he had feared, his brother's expression grew darker.

I guess she told him they could never get married, not as long as he's in the Confederate army, Jeff thought. He felt sorry for Tom, as he had felt sorry for Sarah when she had given him the letter, saying, "Give this to your brother, Jeff, and tell him— well, I've said it all in the letter."

Tom folded his letter, stuck it in his pocket, and turned away, muttering, "I'll see you later." Then he left the tent.

Their father looked after him. "I guess he got bad news from Sarah. I feel bad about those two."

"I do too."

"And Leah, she's all right?"

"Oh, yes. She and her father are going to be sutlers. They're going to follow the Union army."

"That's what Dan says in this letter. Kind of an odd job for a young girl—but I guess it's best. Dan's not in good health, and Leah always was his best nurse." He folded the letter, put it in his pocket, and gave Jeff a fond look. "Well, I'm glad you're back, son. I've missed you."

"When will the army be moving out, Pa?"

"Nobody knows, but it won't be long." His father frowned and shook his head. "I hate to leave you all crowded up with the sergeant's family, but there's not much else I can do about it."

"Pa," Jeff said, a determined look coming to his eyes, "I've got to talk to you."

The seriousness of his son's voice brought the lieutenant's eyes to bear on him. "Why, sure, Jeff, what is it?"

"I know you think I'm too young," Jeff said, "but, Pa, I can't stay here in Richmond."

"You want to go back to Kentucky?"

"Oh, no, I couldn't do that," he protested quickly. He hesitated, then said, "Pa, I want to join the army with you and Tom."

At once his father shook his head. His lips became very tight, and he exclaimed, "No, that's out of the question. You're too young, Jeff. We're not taking anybody in the army under eighteen."

"That's not so, Pa. You know as well as I do that lots of young fellows are telling lies about their ages."

"I can't help that. They're not my sons, and you are."

"Look, Pa, think about me for a minute. What am I going to do staying here in Richmond? I don't know anybody. I'd go crazy."

"I know, son, but—"

"I'm not talking about enlisting as a regular soldier, Pa." Jeff had practiced this speech many times, and now it tumbled out of him. His face was earnest. "I know I couldn't be in the company like Tom, but I could be a drummer boy."

The eyebrows of the older Majors went up. "A drummer boy?"

"Sure, Pa," Jeff said eagerly. "You know they're taking drummer boys in all the time, some of them no more than thirteen. And I'm already fourteen going on fifteen. I can do it, Pa!"

Nelson Majors stood looking across at the earnest face of this younger son of his. He had spent sleepless nights worrying what to do about the boy. He had hoped Jeff would choose to go back and stay with the Carters in Kentucky. But he knew that staying in that environment would be intolerable while his family was fighting on the Southern side. Now as he watched Jeff, he saw clearly the anguish that was in the boy. Still he hesitated.

Jeff finally said, "Don't you see, Pa? I just got to do it! I can't stay here away from you. You and Tom, why, you're all I got."

Biting his lip, Jeff's father stared down at the floor, unable to meet his son's eyes.

Silence fell on the tent, and Jeff was wise enough to know that he needed to say no more. His father, he well understood, was a firm man. Jeff had made his plea, and all he could do was hold his breath and pray that his father would see it his way.

Finally, Lieutenant Majors lifted his eyes. There was a heaviness in them and a strain around his lips. He looked tired, but he said evenly, "Well, Jeff, I don't think there is any good answer for a thing like this. I see your side of it. If I was a boy your age, I'd ask for exactly the same thing." He stared at the boy. "All right, you can enlist as a drummer boy. But that means you beat a drum—that's all. No fighting. You understand?"

"Oh, I understand, Pa. I'll do just what you say."

Jeff saw the worry on his father's face. "Pa, don't worry no more than you can help. I'll be all right. You and Tom are the ones that will be doing the fighting. I'll just be beating the drum."

"That's not exactly right," his father said. "Those drums are to direct men into position, and to do that you've got to be close enough for them to hear them. That means you'll be not far behind the front line, maybe right on it. So you'll be running the same chance as the rest of us."

"I'm not afraid, Pa," Jeff said stoutly. "We'll be all right."

Nelson Majors felt for the first time the weight of all this war meant. He had understood that he must lay his own life on the line, and when his older son had volunteered it had come as no great shock. Tom was of the age when he would do such a thing. But now, looking at this youthful son of his, only fourteen, the blackest hair of all of them—tall for his age, but still only fourteen—*God help me*, he thought. *I've got to do it.*

"Well—" he summoned up a grin and threw his arm around Jeff's shoulders "—let's go find the adjutant. And don't expect any favors out of me, you understand? You and Tom are on your own." He hesitated, then said, "We'll have to pray for each other, Jeff. You and me and Tom, we're going to go through a hard time. We'll have to trust the Lord to keep us."

Jeff was so excited he could hardly think. His black eyes sparkled, and despite himself he grinned. He felt the weight of his father's arm on his shoulders and was excited about the prospect of putting on a uniform and marching with his father and his brother and the others.

"Come on, Pa, let's go. I can't wait till I get that drum and start to beat on it!"

9
A Brand New Army

When the war first began, both the North and the South had recruitment rules that banned boys from joining and fighting. The Union held that a recruit had to be at least eighteen, and the South held approximately that same line. In spite of all this, a tall fourteen- or fifteen-year-old could easily bluff his way past a recruiting sergeant.

By far the easiest way for a boy to slip into the army was as a musician—especially as a drummer or a bugler. These were considered nonfighting positions, so a recruiter often allowed a boy to sign on without worrying about his age. The Union army alone had need of more than 40,000 musicians, while an estimated 20,000 served for the South.

Jeff discovered that many of the lads who joined as drummers and musicians were younger even than he.

He also discovered that the South was not ready to fight a war. He and the other recruits found themselves marching in their street clothes, using wooden guns and even cornstalks for training. One lucky unit might find itself outfitted by the proud citizens of its town. However, this produced a rainbow of uniform colors and styles on both sides. One regiment called itself The Highlands and proudly marched off wearing kilts!

The South's economic power lay in its production of cotton, not in manufacturing. When President Lincoln ordered a complete blockade of all Southern ports, problems in the South multiplied. No wonder recruitment posters made very clear that "volunteers furnish their own clothes."

The result was a hodge-podge of colors in the Confederate army. Once, while watching a group of new recruits drilling, Lieutenant Majors remarked, "It looks like a circus parade and not a serious army."

When uniforms finally did arrive for Jeff and his fellow drummers, the result was not completely pleasing. Jeff found that his trousers were too long by three or four inches. The shirt was coarse, too large at the neck, and too short elsewhere. The cap was an ungainly bag with a pasteboard top and a leather visor—and the overcoat made him feel like a little nubbin of corn in a large husk!

"Why, I can't wear this!" Jeff exclaimed.

Tom laughed. "You fellows just exchange around. Better still, get Pa to take you to a tailor downtown."

Jeff began a campaign at once, and his father agreed when he saw the poorly fitting uniform. After a trip to the tailor, Jeff came back wearing a natty uniform of which he was very proud.

But getting the uniform was only the first step. Once outfitted, the real problems would start.

"Now," Tom said, "you've got to learn how to be a soldier."

Both armies needed soldiers who could be moved quickly and precisely during battle. A long column of marching men might have to be positioned to face an enemy approaching head-on. This could happen in thick woods, or at night, or even in a downpour. And once positioned, the men might have to be repositioned many times to defend against attacks from behind or to move to another spot on the battlefield. To avoid chaos, even a retreat was supposed to be orderly.

The sergeant of A Company, a short, muscular man from Alabama named Holmes, spoke his opinion bluntly. "You've got to get these movements down to where you do them without thinking. I know you boys don't like to drill—but these drills are going to save your lives when we get into battle."

In truth, Jeff handled the marching drills easily, as did his fellows. They were young, healthy, lean, and energetic. And Jeff was pleased to find that as far as marching was concerned, he could keep up with any of the older men.

On the first hard march, one of the large soldiers, who had been giving the boys a hard time, played out.

Jeff received a thrill to see him lying beside the road, gasping for breath, and he could not resist the urge to say, "Hey, big man, come on! We'll never get to Washington with you lying there resting like that!"

Later, Jeff was to be sorry for that.

Curly Henson was the soldier's name. He was a brawny fellow with red hair and a fiery temper. The day after the march, Curly stopped Jeff outside the mess hall, grabbed him by the collar, and pulled him up almost on his toes. "You had a pretty good time making fun of me on that march, didn't you, kid?"

Jeff squirmed in his grasp but was powerless in the large man's hands. When the soldier reached out and cuffed him across the jaw, he gasped but said nothing.

Henson shoved him away so that he fell sprawling. "Now, that's lesson number one." He grinned. "You'll get a few more as time goes on."

Tom had been made a sergeant, and he observed the incident. He came up and helped Jeff to his feet. "What did you do to Henson?"

"Oh, I guess I made fun of him for falling down on the march."

"Well, he's going to make life miserable for you. I guess I had better talk to him for you."

"Don't do that," Jeff said quickly. "It wouldn't be right. I'll take care of myself."

Tom stared at him. "If he gets too rough, come and tell me about it."

It did get rough during the next few days. Curly Henson never missed an opportunity to humiliate the boy. He found opportunities to ridicule him in drill and to trip him as he was walking with his mess kit in his hand, so that he spilled his supper. Each time Henson laughed loudly and said, "Well, you learn how to keep your mouth shut yet, Majors?"

Finally, Jeff could stand it no more. *I've got to get him off of me. He'll make my life miserable if I don't,* he said to himself. And lying at night in his bunk, he thought up a plan. He knew that he was no match for the young man in a fistfight, so he determined on a rather rash action.

The next day he kept a watchful eye on Curly, and, sure enough, the big man sauntered over after breakfast and tipped his coffee cup so that it spilled down the front of Jeff's uniform. "Hey, look how clumsy this kid is. Can't even drink his coffee without spilling it."

Jeff had been sitting down. He rose quickly and noticed that all the other soldiers were keeping an eye on him. They had been well aware of Curly's persecution. With his heart beating fast, Jeff reached over and picked up two muskets with bayonets attached. He tossed one of them toward Henson, who caught it, blinking in surprise and calling out, "Hey, Jeff, stop."

Jeff raised his musket, its bright bayonet pointed right at Henson. "I can't beat you with fists, so let's try it this way, Henson."

A mutter went up from the men, and one of them said, "Don't do it, Jeff."

Henson looked at the bright tip of the bayonet, and Jeff saw fear in his eyes.

Jeff took a step forward. "We've got an even chance this way. You stick me, or I'll stick you—so let's go at it." He took one more step and lifted the bayonet as if to thrust it forward.

Henson yelled, "Hey, some of you stop this kid! I don't want to hurt him!"

Suddenly Tom was there. He said, "Go on, Henson. You've been pushing the boy around. Let's see if you can take it."

Henson blinked as he saw the face of Tom Majors, and he muttered, "Aw, Sarge, I was just having a bit of fun." He tried to grin weakly and said, "I don't want to."

"You've had your fun, Curly," Tom said. He was as tall as Henson and almost as heavy. "I didn't say anything because I didn't want to show favoritism. But the next time you get out of line, we'll just see how well you stand up to a bayonet."

Henson swallowed, turned, and walked away quickly.

Tom turned to Jeff and said, "Well, Private, I don't think you'll have any more trouble from him."

Jeff looked around and saw the admiring looks from the other drummer boys and some of the older men as well. He said, "I hope not, Sarge."

Later, when he was alone with his father, Jeff said, "I didn't know what else to do, Pa. He was making life miserable for me."

"I hate that it came to such a thing. There's some men," his father said harshly, "that are born bullies. Henson's one of them, I suppose, but from what Tom said, I don't think you'll have any more trouble."

That incident was the one sour note in Jeff's training.

He spent hours practicing the drum calls along with the other boys and discovered that he had enough musical ability to learn the signals quite easily. It became a pleasure to him to rattle the drums loudly.

Once, the teacher, a grizzled sergeant, came by and said, "Majors, you're doing fine. Got a natural flair for beating on that drum."

"Why, thank you, Sergeant." Jeff felt the warmth of the compliment. "I aim to do the best that I can."

As time wore on, he became adept at long marches and at executing the commands of the officers. He won the approval of his father and even of one far more important individual.

President Jefferson Davis came to review the troops, and Jeff proudly marched by, rolling the drums along with Company A. He got a good look at the president, a tall man with a lean, drawn face. He remembered hearing that the president was not in good health and thought, *He looks kind of weak. We sure don't need a sick man for president of the Confederacy.*

Later in the day, the commanders of the various units came to review their troops, and newly promoted General Thomas Jackson walked along, greeting each lieutenant and commenting on his company.

When he came to Company A, he said, "Lieutenant Majors, it's a pleasure to see you."

Nelson Majors returned the salute sharply. "I'm glad to see you again, General. This is a good company we have here. I hope you'll come to be proud of it."

Jackson was a tall man with a stoop, and again he wore a forage cap pulled down nearly over his eyes. His uniform was not new—it looked almost shabby. He glanced over the company that was drawn up to attention, and he nodded. They looked very fit. "I'm sure you've done a good job, Lieutenant Majors."

At that moment, Jefferson Davis arrived with a group of the Cabinet, who had been speaking with soldiers down the line.

General Jackson said, "Mr. President, this is Lieutenant Majors, one of our fine engineers who came from Kentucky to join the regiment. And I believe this is his son. Isn't that right, Lieutenant?"

"Yes, Mr. President. This is my son, Tom, a sergeant in the company, and my youngest son, Jeff, who's become a fine drummer boy."

Jefferson Davis had a lean, cadaverous look, but his eyes lit up. "Fine! I congratulate you, sir, on your contribution to your country." He shook hands with Nelson Majors, then with Tom, and finally turned to Jeff. "And you, young man—you've enlisted for a soldier. How old are you, my boy?"

"Almost fifteen," Jeff said quickly.

Jefferson Davis's hand was almost skeleton lean, but it was very strong as he shook Jeff's hand. "Bless you, my boy. May the Lord watch over you and keep you safe. And both of you as well," he said to Lieutenant Majors and Tom.

The visitors moved along, and when the company was dismissed, Jeff said, "I got a letter from Leah. She told about meeting President Lincoln." He grinned at his father. "Now I can tell her she's not the only one who's ever met a president."

* * *

The days stretched on, filled with boredom and monotony for most—marching and drilling and practicing—but to Jeff these things were exciting. He did not have time to write a letter to Leah for a while. But a week after meeting the president, he sat down and wrote,

> Dear Leah,
>
> I got your letter. It was exciting your getting to meet President Lincoln, but I have news too. A few days ago, President Jefferson Davis reviewed our company, and I shook hands with him, Leah. Isn't that something, you and I meeting the presidents of our country?

He bit the end of his pen and tried to think of something personal to say. Finally, he wrote,

> This is all the exciting news, but I have to tell you I'm a little bit scared, Leah. I think everybody is. Nobody wants to admit it, but I'm wondering

what I'll do when the bullets start flying. Pa said every soldier is a little worried about that. I worry about you some too. You be sure you and your pa stay well back. I don't think I could stand it if anything happened to you, Leah. After all, we're best friends and always will be.

He put down the pen, folded the letter, put it in an envelope, and went to give it to his father. "Pa, could you see that this gets sent?"

His father saw the name and address, and he nodded. "I'll be glad to, son. I'm writing to Leah's mother to find out about Esther."

The sound of drilling came to them, sergeants shouting commands, and from far away hoofbeats and the shouts of artillery men as they pulled cannons across the open field.

"Pa, do you think we'll be going to fight soon?"

"I'm afraid so." His father reached over and put his hand on Jeff's shoulder. "When the fighting starts, you keep your head down. I wouldn't want anything to happen to you, Jeff."

Jeff nodded and answered, "You too, Pa."

They both knew that in a battle a bullet had no eyes—either one of them and Tom also could be killed or wounded. But they did not speak of that, and as Jeff left he was once again filled with apprehension as to how he would behave when the bullets started flying.

10

The Army Moves Out

A whirlwind of activity moved in the Army of Northern Virginia. On July 15 it seemed to Jeff that every soldier, and every regiment, was moving at a furious speed. Jeff himself had little equipment to pull together. He put his clothes in a knapsack along with several sacks of candy and other food he had been warned by the veterans to take. He put in an extra uniform, and then he was ready to go.

"You're lucky you don't have to be carrying all this gear," Curly Henson said, looking at the small load that Jeff carried. The big soldier had not tried to bully Jeff any more but seemed determined to make fun of him whenever he could. He looked down now with disgust at the drum and the drumsticks that composed most of Jeff's load. "You can't kill the enemy with a drumstick," he snorted. Picking up his musket he held it in his big hands and grinned. "This is what a *real* soldier carries!"

Charlie Bowers was the smallest drummer in the service. He was a friendly boy of thirteen from Arkansas. Charlie was so tiny there had been some difficulty in fitting him out in a uniform. He looked over at Curly Henson and piped up. "If it wasn't for us drummer boys, you soldiers wouldn't know which way to go!" He had his drum strung around his neck and gave an expert roll with a flourish. "You can't do that with a musket, can you, Curly?"

Henson mumbled and turned away, saying, "This is some army with a bunch of babies in it like you two!"

After he had stalked off, the two boys left their drums with their other equipment and walked around the camp, watching the soldiers frantically packing. Officers were shouting, and the cavalry were getting their horses saddled. Everywhere there was noise, and a huge cloud of dust rose over the camp.

Finally, the two made their way to the edge of camp where a creek supplied some of the water that they drank. They sat down, pulled off their shoes, and let their feet dangle in the water.

"Wish we could take this creek along with us, Charlie." Jeff grinned. The cool water soothed his tired feet. "I've got a feeling we're going to have sore feet before this day is over. Pa said that General Jackson marches his men so hard and fast that the rest of the army calls them Foot Cavalry."

"Aw, we can do it, Jeff." Charlie grinned back at his friend. He was a cheerful boy, always looking at the bright side of things and, despite his poor upbringing, never seemed to grow discouraged. Suddenly he whispered, "Look, Jeff, look at that big old fish! What is it, do you reckon?"

Jeff looked in the direction of Charlie's gesture and said quietly, "Why, that's a bass, Charlie."

"Boy, I'd like to have him in a frying pan! He must be the biggest bass in the whole world!"

Jeff smiled tolerantly. "Why, no, he don't weigh over a pound or maybe a pound and a half. He looks like a minnow beside old Napoleon."

"Napoleon? Why, he was a general or something, wasn't he?"

"Not that Napoleon." Jeff laughed. "Napoleon is the name I gave to a big fish back where I came from."

"You named a fish? You mean you kept him in a bowl?"

"No, he was in a river," Jeff explained. "Me and Leah used to go down and try to catch him. He sure was a smart one, though."

Charlie picked up a stone, aimed, and threw it. It made a splashing sound when it hit the water, and the bass disappeared suddenly. "Shoot, he's gone!" Charlie said. Then, looking over at Jeff, he asked, "Who's Leah?"

"Oh, just a friend of mine that I had back home."

"Leah sure is a funny name. Was he one of your best friends?"

"Leah's a girl. She grew up on the farm next to mine. I guess she's the best friend I ever had."

Charlie stared at him curiously. "That's funny —your having a girl for a friend, I mean. Mostly I just either tease girls or stay away from them."

Jeff grinned. "I guess I do too with most girls. But Leah was different. Like I said, we grew up together."

"Guess you hated to go off and leave her when you joined the army, didn't you?"

Jeff hesitated, then told Charlie the whole story of how the two families had been separated. He could hear the far-off muffled sound of drums beating and bugles blowing, and the dust cloud over the camp seemed to grow larger. When he ended, he said, "I expect Leah and her Pa are headed this way along with the Union army."

103

Charlie looked at him thoughtfully, plucked a blade of grass from the ground, chewed on it, and then asked, "Well, you can't still be friends with her, can you, Jeff? I mean, after all, she's with the Union army, ain't she?"

The thought had troubled Jeff constantly—not so much about Leah but about other of his friends who were approaching in the Union army to do battle. "I don't know about all that, Charlie. Lots of families have been torn right in two. Why, in some of them the father went to one side, and some of his sons went on the other side." He sighed. "It's just a mess, that's what it is! I wish it was all over."

"Well," Charlie said, "I guess it will be pretty soon. That's what I hear anyway. We'll whip the Yankees and run them back to Washington—and then they'll all give up." Then he added wistfully, "I wish I was old enough to be a real soldier."

Jeff stared at him. "Do you think you could shoot somebody? I mean, after all, killing a man is a real serious thing."

"Well, they're trying to kill us, aren't they?" Charlie demanded. "A man's got to shoot back when he gets shot at, don't he?"

Jeff had gone over it so often in his mind, and still he was confused. He said nothing for a while and then watched the smaller boy, who had found a hole and was putting a slender piece of grass down into it.

Charlie waited carefully, then jerked up the grass blade, and cried, "Look, there's a doodlebug, Jeff. Ain't he a dandy?"

Jeff stared at the small bug that had been extracted from the hole. "What are you going to do with him, Charlie? You can't eat a doodlebug."

"I don't know. Not much use for a doodlebug."
He sat for a while then, watching the cavalry gallop by furiously. "Say Jeff—" he hesitated "—you ever think about . . . maybe you might get shot?"

"Could happen. We'll be right in there with the men when the battle starts. We've got to be close enough for them to hear the drums—and a musket shoots a long way." He looked over at the younger boy. "Are you afraid of getting killed, Charlie?"

"Who, me? Why, I don't never think about it." But there was a troubled light in Charlie's eye. "I figure if it's gonna happen, why, it'll just happen."

"Well, maybe—but God gave us sense to get behind a tree when the bullets start to flying. That is," he added, "if there's a tree to get behind."

"What do you think happens when somebody dies?" Charlie went on. "Do you reckon it's like the preachers say? The good people go to heaven, and the bad people go to hell?"

Jeff got to his feet nervously. "I guess so," he said. The subject disturbed him, and he didn't want to talk about it. "Come on, let's go back into camp. We'll be leaving pretty soon."

The two were greeted by Jeff's father. "We'll be moving out in thirty minutes. You stay close to me, Jeff."

"You think we'll fight the Yankees today, Lieutenant?" Charlie asked.

Lieutenant Majors grinned at the small boy. "I don't think they're that close, but they'll be here soon enough. Now get your drums and let's get this show on the road."

* * *

105

The march had been hard. Jeff was very tired by the time camp was made that night. The army had come fourteen miles. That didn't seem like a long way to Jeff. "But," he said, "it was a long way when you got to carry a knapsack and a drum." Marching with the drum threw him off balance, he discovered. It pulled him forward. He tried different positions. He slung it over his shoulder, but then the sling choked him or cut into his shoulders.

The army had moved in a long, serpentine line down the roads and from time to time had to take to the roadside to avoid the guns being pulled by the horses. Time and again a soldier would ride ahead, yelling, "Clear the roads! Clear the roads!" And when the men had moved to the sides, a troop of cavalry would thunder by—raising dust that choked them—or perhaps it was a group of officers, or one of the big cannons.

They camped that night in a big grove of trees beside a group of farmhouses. Since there were thousands of men, they had to wait in line at the wells, and the officers warned them, "Don't drink all the wells dry. These people have to live here."

Twilight had come, and the pleasing smell of cooking meat came to Jeff. There was no such thing as a single campfire feeding all the men, nor a single cook. The men of each company were assigned to squads of six or seven men. Each squad found its own firewood and cooked its own meals.

After Jeff had eaten, Sergeant Henry Mapes said, "You fellows get ready. There's going to be a service tonight."

"A service?" Curly Henson looked up at him with surprise. "What kind of a service, Sarge?"

"Oh, General Jackson's got a preacher along, so we're all going to go get preached at," Mapes said.

"Not me." Henson shook his head stubbornly. "I got preached at enough when I was home. My pa always made me go. Count me out, Sarge."

"I ain't counting nobody out, Curly," the sergeant said sharply. "We're all going to go hear that preaching. The general wants it, and what General Jackson wants, we're going to give him."

That was the end of the argument. After the dishes were washed and the gear put away, Jeff's squad joined others walking over to a large clearing where already a large number of men had gathered.

Jeff saw his father standing beside the general, and he nudged the sergeant. "Look, Sarge. There he is. That's General Jackson. I met him one time."

"Did you now?" the sergeant asked curiously. "Well, I hope he's better than his reputation." He looked across to where Jackson was standing upright and said, "Some of the officers call him Tomfool Jackson. He was an instructor at West Point, but I never heard of him doing much fighting except maybe in the Mexican War."

"Well, we'll find out what kind of soldier he is pretty soon, I reckon," Curly said. He was irritable over being forced to attend the service. "He sure don't look like much!"

Jackson was wearing an old uniform and, as usual, had his forage cap pulled down over his eyes. But as the service went on, he took the cap off, laid it down, and joined in the singing.

Jeff was surprised to find that the songs were those he had heard at his church back in Kentucky.

He sang along but noticed that Curly Henson kept his mouth closed and stubbornly refused to take part.

Finally the singing was over, and General Jackson raised his voice. "I'm glad you've all come to the service tonight, men. We'll be going into battle soon, and I wanted you to have an opportunity to hear the gospel before that happens." He hesitated, then said, "I am no preacher—just a simple soldier. But one thing I have discovered is that God is real and that Jesus Christ is the only answer for the problems that you and I meet. Let me introduce to you Major Phineas Roland, our chaplain."

Roland was a tall, raw-boned man in a brand-new uniform and did not look like most preachers that Jeff had seen. However, he at once said, "I am not a soldier, men. Just a country preacher. General Jackson has been kind enough to allow me to speak to you tonight. So I want to talk to you about the one subject that every man must know about." He opened the thick black Bible he held in his big hands and read one verse. "'Except a man be born again, he cannot see the kingdom of God.'"

Silence fell as the men stood listening. The preacher's voice was high-pitched but pleasant and carried over the crowd easily, so that even those at the back heard him clearly.

"Jesus came to do one thing," Roland said. "'I am come that you may have life, and that you may have it more abundantly.'

"All of us right now are alive," he said. "At least we're living, breathing, eating, and sleeping. But Jesus said there's more to life than those things. He said a man has to come to know God, or he will never amount to anything." The preacher went on

108

talking about how people needed a life aside from physical life.

"If you're not born again, you're not right with God," he said firmly. "And how does a man get to be born again? Jesus said it was like the wind—you can't explain it. But the rest of the Bible is devoted to telling us about that." He told how a person needed to repent of his sins and call upon God through Jesus Christ. Finally, he said, "I'm asking you to do that right now. If there's a man here who knows he's not right with God, I beg you to come and let me pray with you. It won't take but one minute for you to get right with God. But you'll have all eternity, if you're not, to regret your condition."

The men began to sing, and several soldiers started to move forward. Jeff felt uncomfortable, but he did not move. Then he looked up in surprise to see Charlie Bowers walk forward with the older soldiers.

Jeff watched as little Charlie stood there, and finally the big chaplain noticed him. He bent over, and the two talked for a long time. Then Jeff saw Charlie bow his head as the chaplain put his hands on the boy's shoulders.

"Well, look at that!" Curly Henson grinned. "It looks like your friend is going to hit the glory road, don't it, Jeff?"

Jeff didn't answer.

When the service was over, Charlie came back. He could hardly talk, he was so filled with emotion. His eyes were bright with tears, and his voice shook. "Jeff—hey, Jeff! I just got saved."

"Did you, Charlie? That's good. I'm glad for you."

The two walked back toward where they were camped, and for a long time they lay awake in their little tent as Charlie talked about what had happened to him. Finally, he said, "Jeff, are you saved?"

Silence ran between the two for a moment. Then, "I don't reckon so, Charlie. Nothing like that ever happened to me."

Charlie raised up on one elbow to see the face of his friend by the moonlight. "You better get saved," he urged. "Like you said, either one of us could get killed tomorrow."

Jeff thought about that. "I guess it just hasn't come to me yet," he said, then closed his eyes. He knew that Charlie wanted to talk more, but he didn't want to hear it.

Finally he drifted off into a fitful sleep, wondering what it really meant to be "born again."

* * *

The army arose before dawn and after a quick breakfast was on the road. All morning long Jeff moved forward, choking on the dust, and finally was relieved to hear Sergeant Mapes say, "All right, we're here."

Jeff looked ahead to see the army pulling itself into a line. Down below he saw a creek. "What's the name of that creek, Sergeant Mapes?"

"They call it Bull Run," Mapes said, staring down at the little stream. He lifted his eyes and tried to stare into the distance beyond. "I reckon the Yankees are somewhere on the other side there. They'll be coming at us today or tomorrow."

The Yankees did not come that day, however, and that night at supper Jeff was glad to see Tom come walking over.

Tom was with a different platoon but sat down for a while and ate a piece of the bacon that Jeff was working on. After a while he looked over in the darkness toward where the enemy lay. "I want you to do me a favor, Jeff."

"Sure, what is it, Tom?"

Tom reached into his pocket and pulled out a letter. "This is for Sarah," he said, "in case I—in case something happens to me."

Jeff took the letter uncomfortably. "Aw, nothing's going to happen to you, Tom. You'll be all right."

"Why, sure." Tom grinned back. "Just a little insurance, you know. Anyway, you see it gets to Sarah if something does happen."

Jeff pushed the letter into his knapsack, and the two sat there in the quietness of the night, broken only by the sound of soldiers up and down the line of battle, murmuring.

Finally Tom said, "You know, it hurts me to think that one of those fellows we'll be shooting at tomorrow—it could be Royal." He chewed his lip nervously. "What if I kill Sarah's brother? That's the worse thing I can think of."

Jeff said quickly, "Oh, Tom, there's not much chance of that. They've got a big army over there. Why, it'd be a strange thing if you two even saw each other."

Tom took a deep breath and then nodded. "I guess I'll just have to think like that." He leaned over and slapped Jeff on the shoulder. "You take care of yourself tomorrow, little brother. Don't want anything to happen to you."

"You too, Tom. You'll be right up where the fighting is, I guess. You and Pa." Jeff had not intended to say anything, but now in the quietness he found it was possible. "Tom," he said, "I hate to tell you this, but I'm downright scared."

Tom laughed and waved his arm around at the line of soldiers, at the flickering line of campfires that winked like red eyes in the darkness. "You ask any one of those fellows, Jeff, on either side" —he indicated the Yankee line off in the far distance— "and they'll all tell you the same thing. We're all of us scared. No man likes to think about getting wounded or maimed or maybe dying."

The two of them sat there for a long time, and finally Tom got up. He reached down and ruffled Jeff's hair. "Good night, Jeff. You watch yourself tomorrow."

He walked off into the darkness. And as he did, Jeff felt lonely. He wanted to go to his father but knew that would not be right, since his father had many men to see to.

Finally he went to bed, and the last thing he remembered was Charlie saying, "Sure am glad I got saved, Jeff!"

11

A Sort of Holiday

The Army of the Potomac approached their first battle with a holiday spirit. Daniel Carter and Leah had loaded their wagon, packed all their supplies, then stood to one side watching as the troops moved out. The marching army made an informal parade, and despite the efforts of the professional soldiers the new recruits seemed to feel that the whole thing was a lark.

"Look at that, Pa! They act like they're going out for a Sunday picnic!" Leah said indignantly.

Ira Pickens, who had come to say good-bye while his unit formed, grinned at Leah. "I reckon that's the way it is, Miss Leah. We've heard so much about how easy this is going to be, why, the fellers they think it'll just be a bit of fun."

Mr. Carter's face was even thinner than usual. The heat of summer and the hardship of camping out had worn him down. But his mouth was firm under his striking mustache. "I don't reckon it's going to be much fun, Ira. Some of those men are headed for their graves and don't know it."

A shiver went down Leah's back. She looked up at her father quickly, noting the sadness in his face. Then she turned her eyes back to the parade. "Look—there's Royal's company! Do you see him, Pa?"

The blue-clad soldiers marched proudly by, and her father suddenly pointed. "There he is—in the

113

third line back. Do you see him, Leah? Don't he look fine, though?"

Leah searched the troop and was thrilled to see her brother. "Royal! Royal!" she cried as he marched by. Her high voice carried over the sounds of the singing.

Royal turned to face her, grinned, and gave her a little salute as the company passed.

"Well, I better get back to my outfit," Ira said. He hesitated, then said, "I sure do thank you for writing those letters to that sweetheart of mine, Leah."

"Oh, you'll be writing them yourself pretty soon." Leah smiled at him encouragingly. "You be careful, now. Don't get hurt."

"Oh, I never get hurt," Ira said, waving his hand airily. "Good-bye, Mr. Carter. You stay close with that wagon of yours, because the boys are sure going to want to celebrate after we whup the Rebels."

The young man hurried off, and Leah's father watched him sadly. "He doesn't have any idea what he's headed into," he murmured. "I don't think any of them do."

"Well, Pa, let's go get the wagon. We'll have to be on our way and follow the army."

"I guess so, daughter."

The two of them went back to the wagon and spent some time making sure that everything breakable was carefully packed.

Finally, late that afternoon, the last of the troops went by. "I guess we can get in behind them," Mr. Carter said. "We're going to have to eat dust, though."

They had to do exactly that. Outside Washington the dirt roads, dried by summer's heat, threw up a fine yellow cloud that settled on their hair and got into their eyes. They stayed a few miles behind the last of the troops but discovered that some late-appearing soldiers marched past them.

"Those are some of the ninety-day men, I guess." Her father nodded at the young men as they went by. "Some of them are just afraid they'll miss out on the fighting—but I don't think they have to worry about that."

Leah watched and once again thought how light-hearted they were. They were singing at the top of their lungs one of the songs they had learned in the camp:

"With stars and stripes and martial glee,
    We'll send Jeff Davis up a tree;
    His traitorous band must follow suit,
    Because they like that kind of fruit.

"Get out of the way, old Jeff Davis,
    Out of the way, old Jeff Davis,
    Out of the way, old Jeff Davis,
    You're too late to come to enslave me!"

Time and again they broke ranks, despite their sergeant's curses, and dashed off into the woods to get a drink of water from a meandering creek. Some found a blackberry patch, and when they called, "Come on, fellows! Here's dessert!" the whole squad ran. Soon the berry patch was filled with shouting, frolicking, blue-clad soldiers.

Mr. Carter pulled up his wagon to watch them and turned to Leah. "Maybe you better get some of those blackberries for us. They wouldn't go down bad."

Leah said, "All right, Pa." Grabbing a bucket out of the wagon, she leaped to the ground and soon the rich, plump fruit was striking the bottom of her bucket with a drumming sound.

A young soldier came up, his mouth berry-stained. "Hey, missy," he said with a wide grin, "you going to the battle?"

"My pa and I, we're sutlers," she said. She looked him over carefully. He seemed to be no more than sixteen or seventeen. "Aren't you afraid you'll get separated?"

"Why, we're headed right toward Centerville. I know it as well as I know my own front door," he said and waved jauntily. "As a matter of fact, I live only ten miles over thataway. From what I hear, the Rebels are holed up at Centerville. We'll hit them there and run them all the way back to Richmond!"

"I wish you good luck," Leah said.

"Aw, we'll be all right," the young soldier said. "Here, let me help you fill that bucket up." He was a quick-moving young man, and soon Leah's bucket was filled with the juicy fruit. He grinned again and said, "I wish you good luck too, missy. You be careful now. Stay back when the fighting starts."

Leah moved back to the wagon, climbed on board, and offered the fruit to her father.

He took a berry, looked at it, and put it into his mouth. "My," he said, "that is good! Always was partial to a fresh berry."

They ate slowly, laughing as the sergeants and corporals went into the blackberry patch to rout the wandering soldiers back onto the road.

"They'll have chiggers all over 'em, I bet," Leah said. "Some of them act like they've never been in a blackberry patch. Chiggers and blackberries just go together, don't they?"

"They sure do." Her father took another berry and chewed it thoughtfully. "I'm worried about Royal. Just can't help it, Leah. When the battle starts, there's no telling what'll happen." He spoke to the horses then, and they moved forward again.

When they got to Centerville they discovered that the Rebels had pulled back. "There won't be any battle here today," Ira Pickens said. His regiment was camping just outside of the town, and he had come back to find them. "But I reckon they'll be right ahead of us tomorrow."

"Come on and eat supper with us," Leah said. "Maybe I can get one more letter off to that sweetheart of yours."

"Sounds good to me," Ira said eagerly. "Just a minute—I've got something for you."

He disappeared and was back shortly carrying a chicken, whose neck had been wrung. Holding it up, he said, "I liberated this here bird."

"Ira, you *stole* that chicken!"

"I did not neither," he exclaimed indignantly. "I found it."

Leah could not help laughing. "I know where you found it too. In some poor farmer's chicken yard! He'll be lucky if he's got a chicken left after this bunch gets by!"

Nevertheless, she took the bird and plucked and dressed it. That night they had a fine supper of fried chicken and baked potatoes.

Ira left shortly afterward, saying, "The sergeant said if we're not back he's going to pull all our hair out or worse. So I'll see you tomorrow."

The next morning the army began to move early, and as they left Centerville her father looked back. "Look at what's coming, Leah," he said.

Several fine carriages were approaching.

"My, who are they, Pa?"

"That man in the front's a congressman. I heard him make a speech once."

The carriages passed. The fine horses were going at practically a gallop.

When they were gone, he said, "Those men are foolish! Why, they've got their wives and children with them!"

"And they've got picnic baskets too. They're just going out to see the battle like it was some kind of entertainment." She was indignant. "I don't think that's right, Pa."

"No, it's not, and it's not wise either. A man would be a fool to take little children out to a thing like this."

The procession slowed down late that afternoon, and finally they saw that the army was pitching camp again.

Later, as they were cooking supper, Royal came by. "You got anything to eat?" he said with a grin. "All we've got is hardtack. Make a man break a tooth trying to chew it."

"You sit down, and I'll cook you the best supper you've ever had," Leah said firmly. She began scurrying around, collecting the elements for a meal.

Soon Royal said, "Boy, that smells good." And finally, when it was put before him, he ate ravenously.

"You hear any talk about the Rebels?" their father asked. "All we hear is gossip back here."

Royal shrugged his shoulders. "Well, that's

about all we get up front too. But ahead of us a little ways there's a creek, a little stream called Bull Run. What the officers say is that the Rebels have pulled back across Bull Run Creek and are just waiting for us. Guess we'll hit 'em first thing in the morning."

Mr. Carter picked up a stick and began to stir the hot coals under the coffeepot. They broke into flames, and the three of them watched for a while.

Finally Royal said, "You two stay well back out of this. Those cannon can fire a mile, I guess. Wouldn't want you to get hurt."

Leah said impulsively, "I wish you were out of it too, Royal."

"Well, I'm not. We're in it for sure now." He appeared gloomy and sipped the coffee that she gave him, silent for a long time. "I hope this settles it. Maybe if we whip 'em bad enough they'll realize that they can't stand up against us. From what I hear, a lot of people in the South didn't want this war anyway."

"I wish that would happen," their father said.

He looked sickly in the feeble flickering of the small fire, his face lined. He had eaten practically nothing, Leah noticed, which was a bad sign.

"I worry about you, Royal, and the other boys from our town." He peered hard into the darkness ahead. "I worry about those other boys too. And about the Majorses. I sure would hate for anything to happen to them."

Leah passed around the can of blackberries for dessert.

As they ate, Royal said, rather awkwardly, "Well, I guess this might sound funny, but there's something I want to say."

"What is it, son?"

Royal appeared to have lost his appetite. He looked into the fire for a long time, then up at the others. "I'm not expecting anything to happen, you know. But just in case something does, Pa, I want to tell you what a good father you've been to me. You and Ma—why no boy had better parents!"

Something about the way he spoke frightened Leah, but she could say nothing. A huge lump was in her throat at the very idea that Royal might be killed, and she had to blink back tears.

Royal, seeing his father and sister staring at him, said quickly, "Well, I might as well say it. I might not make it tomorrow. Some of us sure won't, if we tangle with the Rebs." He straightened and nodded firmly, "But if I don't make it, I want you to know I'll be with Jesus. I'm not afraid to die, but —like every man, I guess—I'd miss you, my family, and the things I always planned on doing. If I have to die for our country, I'll do it. But we won't lose. God's on our side."

Leah was moved by his words. Later, after Royal had left, she said, "Pa, is that right—that God's on our side?"

"Well, we would like to think that," her father said slowly. "Why," he asked, "don't you think He is?"

Leah looked off into the darkness where her brother had disappeared, then farther off to where she knew the enemy troops lay. "I don't know, Pa. I'm pretty sure there are people over there thinking God's on their side. So I just don't know."

Leah was depressed by the thought of the impending conflict. She went to bed but did not sleep well—wondering about and dreading the battle that would take place the next day.

12

There Stands Jackson
Like a Stone Wall!

The two armies that lay on opposite sides of Bull Run Creek were amateurs at the art of war. The Northern commander, General Irving McDowell, reported in disgust, "[The troops] stopped every moment to pick blackberries or get water; they would not keep in ranks, or do as much as you please. When they came where water was fresh, they would pour the old water out of their canteens and fill them with fresh water. They were not used to denying themselves much; they were not used to journeys on foot."

Thus it was that when the main column of Union troops passed through a small town called Fairfax, the heat and fatigue of the day's march had not dimmed their high spirits. They ransacked the neighborhood for milk, butter, eggs, and poultry. Here and there a stray shot echoed where a soldier had killed not a deer but one of the cattle that were quietly grazing. There was even some sportive barn-burning—and vandalizing and torching of homes from which the occupants had fled.

But soon enough that aspect of the affair ceased, and the Union troops were thrown against the ground occupied by Confederate General Beauregard's center.

Suddenly a volley of gunfire came from the

green foliage, startling Royal, and the air was thick, he thought, with leaden rain. A white cloud rose above the trees, and a wild yell like the whoop of war-painted Indians was heard above the din of battle as General Longstreet's brigade delivered the first round and sent up its first battle cry.

Colonel William Tecumseh Sherman, soon to be promoted to general and later to be the right-hand man of General Grant, said afterward, "For the first time in my life I saw cannonball strike men and crash through the trees and saplings above us and around us."

Royal turned to look his squad over and saw that they were very apprehensive.

The lieutenant came by. "Royal, watch the men. They're not used to this. They may try to run."

Royal forced a smile. "Well, who's going to watch me, Lieutenant? I guess you better do that."

The lieutenant shook his head. "No, I'm not worried about you. What I'm worried about is Joe Johnston."

"Who's he? Oh, you mean the Confederate general?"

The lieutenant shaded his eyes with his hands and said, "He's supposed to be camped over in the Shenandoah Valley by our General Patterson. But if he gets away and joins this fight, we're going to have a hard time."

What the lieutenant did not know was that General Joseph Johnston had already managed to elude the Federals under General Patterson and had moved two-thirds of his troops by train partway to the Bull Run lines. It was the first time in history that soldiers had been transported to a battlefield by rail.

Back of the lines, Leah and her father had watched the troops nervously preparing for battle. Soon after the firing started, Dan Carter looked up in surprise. "Why, look—there's some of our boys coming back. Wonder why they're not going forward?"

The troops marched by, and one soldier stopped to buy some food. As Mr. Carter provided it, he asked, "Where are you going? The battle's that way."

The soldier, a short, overweight man with a sunburned face, said, "We're three months' volunteers, and our enlistment just ran out. We're headed back to town."

"Well, I think that's awful," Leah burst out. "Leaving your comrades to fight the battle alone."

The fat soldier looked at her in embarrassment. "Well," he said, "we done our fighting at Blackburn's Ford. Now let the rest of them take over." He turned and walked away.

Not long after that, they saw more carriages bringing the civilians who had driven out from Washington to witness the operations. One of the nearby sutlers said, "There's our senator." And some recognized other members of Congress.

"I still don't think that's right," Dan Carter said stubbornly, "for those men to come out and see a battle like it was a picnic."

* * *

Across the river, General Jackson's corps occupied a position far right of the Union line. Lieutenant Nelson Majors had been assigned as one of Jackson's couriers, and he stayed slightly back as messages came to and fro from the battle.

Finally General Jackson turned and said, "Lieutenant, go see if you can find General Beauregard. Tell him we're not getting any action at all over here on the right. Ask him for orders. See if you can find out what's going on."

"Yes, sir." The lieutenant spurred his horse down the line of Confederates who had taken position behind trees and the logs that they had thrown up overnight. To his left he could hear the sound of musket fire and cannons. Finally, after some difficulty, he found General Beauregard's headquarters.

A major stopped him and inquired about his business.

"General Jackson asked if there were any new orders. He says there's no activity over to the right."

At that moment a group of officers rode up, and the major said, "Wait a minute. Here's General Johnston, just come from the Shenandoah Valley. Maybe he'll know what's going on."

General Johnston took General Beauregard's salute.

"I'm glad to see you, General," Beauregard said. "Are your men close behind?"

"Most of them are. The rest will be here shortly." General Johnston was a small man, neatly dressed. His uniform was impeccable. "I was expecting to find you engaged in the battle, General Beauregard."

"I had planned," General Beauregard said, "to attack this morning. But then I decided to let the enemy move first. Then we can move our troops to where he hits us."

Johnston looked up and down the lines. "I don't see any signs of an attack." He turned his head slightly and said, "But I hear cannon fire over to the left—and musketry too."

"Yes," Beauregard said, "I've heard the same." He hesitated, apparently not certain what to do. He thought hard for a moment. General Johnston was the ranking officer on the field, so Beauregard suggested, "The battle is there, General. We need to throw our men into it."

Just then Jeff's father spurred his horse forward. Saluting, he said, "General, General Jackson would like orders, sir."

Johnston at once said, "Tell General Jackson I said to move his troops to our left. That's where the enemy seems to be attacking."

"Yes, sir."

Nelson Majors whirled his horse around and drove the animal at a dead run back to his brigade.

As soon as he drew up, he said, "General Jackson. General Johnston has arrived from the Shenandoah. The Yankees are attacking over on the left. He commands you to take your brigade at once to engage them there."

General Jackson's eyes seemed to glow with a pale blue light. He nodded. "Yes, Lieutenant." Then he raised his voice and called out to his staff officers, "Move at once to the left. The enemy is attacking there."

Tom was waiting impatiently, and Jeff came to stand beside him. Jeff was apprehensive and nervous.

Suddenly Tom said, "Look, there's Pa—I mean, there's the lieutenant."

They hurried forward to hear their father cry, "Company A, prepare to march. We're moving to

125

our left. No stragglers now." He glanced over, saw his sons, and said, "Let's hear those drums, drummer boy, and get the men at once to moving."

Jeff called out, "Yes, sir," and began to sound the appropriate drum rolls. Bugles blew, men shouted, and soon it seemed the whole brigade was running toward the left. Ahead he could see General Jackson and his staff as they moved in that direction.

"Shoot!" he gasped as he stumbled along over the rough ground. "I guess we're into it this time!"

Curly Henson's face was rather pale under his sunburn. He had been boastful all night about what he would do to the Yankees, but now he muttered, "I'd just as soon them Yankees turned around and went back to Washington!"

As they approached the left of the Confederate line, the sound of combat swelled. Officers called out orders, and the men were thrown into a battle formation.

Jeff stood close to his father, who continually barked out commands. "Move to the right!" "Get the strikers together!" "Watch them, sergeant! Don't let them shoot until we've got something to shoot at."

Jeff would never forget his first exposure to enemy fire. It sounded as though a giant were breaking huge sticks—*crack! crack! crack! crack!*

The Confederate cannons stationed nearby almost deafened him with their roar as they threw their missiles across Bull Run Creek. All was noise and fire and smoke—and then suddenly, just down the line from him, a soldier coughed loudly, then fell. Two or three of his comrades moved to him, and one looked up with a white face and whispered, "He's dead! Got him right in the heart!"

Jeff's breath seemed to stop. It was as if an iron band were tightened around his chest. He had known the soldier, a young man named Tim Eberly, who came from Mississippi. He had shared a plate of beans once with him and listened to the young man tell about a fox hunt he'd been on.

Fearfully, Jeff looked over at him. There was an awful stillness about him, and his white face frightened Jeff. *Tim's never going to get to go back to Mississippi*, he thought numbly and swallowed hard.

Then amid the booming of cannons and the rattle of musket fire he heard his father call, "Look out—here they come! Every man load, but don't fire until I give the signal!"

Jeff crouched down at his sergeant's command as blue-clad figures emerged from the battle smoke. They were running as fast as they could, it seemed, and Jeff had the impulse to turn and run away. When they were no more than fifty feet away, Jeff's father shouted, "Fire!"

A crash of rifle fire echoed his words, and Jeff saw a huge gap suddenly appear in the blue line. Some men fell. Others were driven back, dropping their muskets. The whole line of unharmed men wavered. Looking around and seeing their predicament, suddenly they whirled and ran back into the smoke.

"We stopped them that time!" Curly Henson gasped. "We sure stopped them Yankees, didn't we?"

But that was merely the first charge. Time and again the blue waves came rushing into the battle, and slowly the Confederates were driven back.

127

"We can't stand this long," Jeff muttered to the sergeant. "Lots of our men have gone down."

The sergeant nodded. "I know it." He paused, then said, "Look! Who's that officer?"

Lieutenant Majors stood up to see more clearly. "I know him. That's General Bee. Looks like they've been taking a beating." Jeff watched as General Bee rode up.

"General Jackson—they're driving us back!"

Jackson, mounted on his horse, looked over at the fury of the battle and shook his head firmly. His eyes blazed. "Then we will give them the bayonet. Stand your ground, sir!"

General Bee seemed to take courage from this. He whirled his horse around, rode back a few yards, and Jeff could hear him call, "Men, don't run!—rally behind the Virginians! There stands Jackson like a stone wall!"

And that was the way General Jackson got his nickname. "I guess now he'll always be Stonewall Jackson," Jeff heard his father say as the Virginians moved forward. He added to Jeff, "I'm glad you're all right. I've got to go forward now. You stay up as much as you can."

"All right, Pa," Jeff said with a swallow. "I'll do like you say. But you be careful, will you?"

But Jeff's father could not be careful. There was no way to be careful in the battle that followed. All afternoon long the cannons roared, and the muskets crackled. Charges and countercharges took place on ground close to a house owned by a family named Henry. Guns were brought into place and began a withering fire. Some were captured and turned upon the enemy.

During one charge, Jeff found himself suddenly left behind as the Confederates were beaten back. He looked up to see a blue-clad Yankee rushing right at him with a bayonet. The man's eyes were insane with battle-madness, and Jeff knew that he could never get away. Nevertheless, he whirled and tried to run. His drum thumped against him.

Then, almost in his ear, a rifle exploded. He turned to see the Union soldier fall—and Curly Henson lower his musket. Curly's face was black with gunpowder.

"You OK, boy?" he asked huskily.

"Sure. I am now." Jeff looked at the Union soldier, then back to Curly. "I guess you saved my bacon that time, Curly. I owe you one."

Curly Henson had given the boy nothing but problems, but somehow that had all changed now. He laid a large, rough hand on Jeff's shoulder and grinned. "Aw, we Rebels got to stick together, don't we? Come on, Jeff, let's get out of this."

13

The Fires of Battle

The Battle of Bull Run developed into a contest for possession of the plateau surrounding the Henry house.

When Lieutenant Nelson Majors climbed to the top of the slight ridge, he had a clear view of the whole line. "Look, there," he said to Sergeant Mapes, "you can see the enemy like bees in a hive."

They watched as the officers rode about and their columns moved about everywhere. Some batteries on the left and right were masked by trees, but the lieutenant could see puffs of smoke and knew that the shells were falling on the North's own lines.

"Not much order over there, is there, Sergeant? Look, those regiments are scattered, and the lines aren't even."

"No, sir, but I guess we've got about as many stragglers as they have." Mapes looked around. "I ain't never seen anything quite this bad. Lots of men have fallen, and that makes some others run away."

"And a lot of men are hurt too." Nelson Majors watched the continuous stream of injured being carried past. Sometimes soldiers would cross their muskets, place their wounded companions across them, and carry them. A wounded soldier walked past with his arm around another soldier's neck, the two of them making their way slowly to the rear.

"This is hard going, Mapes," Lieutenant Majors said. "We're going to have to do better than this if we're going to whip those Yankees."

"I guess you're right, sir—look, the General's motioning for you."

Nelson Majors saw Jackson signaling him to come forward. He moved his horse up beside the General's, and Jackson said, "Lieutenant, I want you to ride from battery to battery and see that the guns are properly aimed and the fuses are the right length."

"Yes, sir." He immediately galloped away to do as the General had ordered.

"We ain't got much ammunition left," one artillery officer told him. "Tell the general if we're going to do anything, we had better do it quick."

Nelson Majors made his way back to General Jackson and gave his report, adding, "The guns are running low on ammunition, General."

Jackson's eyes fairly blazed. He had a way, the lieutenant had noticed, of throwing up his left hand with the open palm toward the person he was addressing. He threw it up now and said, "All right, Lieutenant, we'll—"

Then he jerked his hand down, and the lieutenant saw blood streaming from it.

"General, you're wounded!"

Jackson drew a handkerchief from his breast pocket and began to bind up his hand. "Only a scratch—a mere scratch," he said and galloped away.

The battle raged for another hour, and then General Jackson returned, his staff officers behind him. "We'll be leading a charge, Lieutenant Majors. I want Company A in the front. Are your men ready?"

"Yes, sir."

"Then have your drummer boy signal the charge."

Nelson Majors whirled away and found his top sergeant. "We're going to charge, Mapes." He looked about and saw Jeff. "Jeff, sound the charge."

Jeff's face was pale, but he at once began beating the long drum roll that announced the charge.

At once the men looked up, though weary already with fighting.

Lieutenant Majors drew his saber. "Follow me, men! We've got them this time!"

The entire company moved forward. To their right and to their left, other companies began to form.

Jeff marched along, but the lines became so uneven that it seemed there was little order. He saw his father getting far ahead and wanted to call out to him to slow down.

Curly Henson stayed beside him. "That pa of yours—he don't know what fear is, does he?"

"I wish he did, Curly," Jeff muttered. "He's getting too far ahead."

Even as he spoke, he heard the thunder of Federal artillery. Shells began to drop all around them. One came so close that it almost deafened him, and when the dirt had stopped falling he saw that several men were down.

Then, lifting his eyes, Jeff saw a group of Federal soldiers emerge from a stand of trees. He yelled, "Look out, Pa!"

But he was too late. One of the blue-clad men leveled his musket. A puff of smoke came from the end of it. At almost the same time, Jeff saw his father throw up his hands and go to the ground.

"Pa!" He stripped off his drum and leaped ahead, but Curly Henson threw his arms around him. "It's too late, Jeff," he said. "See—the Yankees have cut us off."

Jeff saw that what the curly-haired man said was true. The Federals who had come out of the trees were joined by others, so that now they formed a solid line. But Jeff still struggled to free himself. "I've got to get to him."

But now the sergeant was yelling, "Retreat! Retreat!"

"Come on, Jeff, your pa will be all right—probably just wounded. He'll be a prisoner, but he'll be OK."

* * *

General Beauregard's face ordinarily was an olive color, but now his officers saw that he had grown pale. When one said, "I don't see how we can go on, sir," the general did not answer.

Suddenly he raised his arm. In the distance a column of men was approaching. "Whose flag is that?" Beauregard demanded.

"I don't know," a major answered. "I can't tell at this distance whether it's Federal or Confederate."

General Beauregard stared at the flag. He well knew that, despite all their efforts, if the men under that flag were Union troops the battle was lost. He took his glass to examine the flag and the approaching banner, but he still could not identify it.

Finally, Colonel Evans said, "I fear that may be Patterson's division from the Valley. If so, it's all up with us, I'm afraid, General Beauregard."

Just then a gust of wind shook out the folds of the flag, and the general shouted, "It's the stars and bars!"

Cheer after cheer was raised along the Confederate lines as the men came on. These were Kirby Smith's troops from the Shenandoah Valley. Their train had broken down, but they had arrived on the field at the supreme moment.

The reinforcements had an extraordinary effect on the battle. They threw themselves into the woods and laid down a withering fire on the Union troops. The Federal soldiers soon disintegrated into disorder. Their officers made every attempt to rally them but in vain, and soon the slopes were swarming with retreating and disorganized forces. Riderless horses and artillery teams ran furiously through the fleeing men.

All further Union efforts were futile. Something had happened to the Army of the Potomac. All sense of manhood seemed forgotten. Even the sentiment of shame had gone. Everything was thrown aside that would hinder flight. Rifles, bayonets, pistols, haversacks, cartridges, canteens, blankets, belts, and overcoats lined the road as they fled.

Daniel Carter and Leah sensed that the battle had turned.

"I think we're losing," he said. As if to confirm his words, a crowd of Union soldiers suddenly appeared over the hillcrest. They carried no guns, and they ran frantically like men in a wild race.

As they passed by, Leah saw that their eyes were blank with fear. No one could have stopped them.

"We'd better get out of here, I guess, Leah," her father said. "If the troops are running, the Confederates will be here soon." He turned the wagon around and followed the Warren Turnpike, which soon became the main line of retreat for soldiers, sutlers, and spectators.

When they reached a bridge, Leah saw that gunfire had taken down a team of horses ahead of them. The wagon had overturned directly in the center of the bridge, and their passage was completely obstructed. Shot and shell from Rebel fire continued to fall, and the infantry were furiously pelted with a shower of grape and other shot. The dead lay all about.

Seeing the bridge blocked, drivers began turning off, and their wagons bumped over the rough stones as they forded the small creek. Army wagons, sutlers' teams, and private carriages choked the passage, tumbling against each other amid clouds of dust. The congressmen whipped their horses furiously. Horses, many of them wounded, galloped at random. Men who could catch them rode them bareback, as much to save themselves from being run over as to make quicker time.

"We'd better pull off, or we'll get trampled," Leah's father said. He drew the wagon to one side, and for some time they watched the troops running pell-mell.

"Look, Pa, there's Ira!" Leah jumped out of the wagon before her father could stop her and ran over to where Ira Pickens was limping along.

He was using his musket for a crutch, and looking down she saw that his right leg was bloodied below the knee. His face was drained white, and his eyes were blank, but when he saw her he seemed to recover himself somewhat.

"Well, didn't expect to see you here," he gasped.

"Ira, you've been shot," Leah cried. She saw that his hands were trembling. "Lean on me," she said. "Our wagon's right over here."

"Reckon I'll take you up on that," he whispered.

She helped him over to the wagon, and her father said, "Lie down here, son, and let me look at that leg."

Ira obediently slipped to the ground as if unable to stand, and Leah forced herself to watch as her father pulled up the trouser leg.

"It's not bad," Dan Carter said quickly. "The bullet went through without breaking a bone, it looks like. But the bleeding's pretty bad. Leah, get one of my shirts, and we'll make a bandage."

Leah jumped into the wagon and frantically grabbed a shirt. Then she tore it into strips and helped as her father made a compress and tied it tightly with long strips of the cloth.

"Sure am thirsty," Ira said. "Never knew a fellow could be so thirsty."

At once Leah got a dipper and drew water out of the barrel fastened to the side of the wagon. "Drink this, Ira," she said, holding it to his lips.

The soldier drank, gulping furiously, and then they helped him to the wagon.

"I guess we can get across now," her father said. He looked back over the field. "It looks like we got whipped, Ira."

Ira too looked back toward the battlefield, where guns were still firing and dust was still rising. Shaking his head, he said, "I thought we had 'em for a while—but then they got lots of help from somewhere. They just plain run over us there at the last." He gritted his teeth and said, "They whupped us this time, but there'll be another day!"

Leah made a pallet for him in the wagon. "Lie down here, Ira," she said. Then she poured a spoonful of liquid from a brown bottle. "Take some of this. It'll help with the pain."

She held his head up, and when he had taken the medicine he lay back again, smiled, and said, "I guess I might as well tell you the truth, Miss Leah."

Leah stared at him. "What's that, Ira?"

"You know that girl Rosie you've been writing all them letters to?"

"Yes, what about her?"

Ira made a face and said, "Well, there ain't no Rosie. I just made her up."

"Why in the world would you do that?"

Ira came up with a smile. The medicine had started to work. He muttered, "Well, I ain't never been able to have a gal of my own, so I thought if I could get you to write letters for me . . . well . . . that'd be almost like having one." He started to say something else, but sleep came upon him, and he fell into deep unconsciousness.

Leah sat beside him and smiled. "I'm glad you made it through all right, Ira," she said. "You'll have a girl of your own someday."

* * *

Nelson Majors came out of warm darkness into a world of shouting and pain. He was aware that his side was one mass of agony, and then suddenly he was being picked up. He opened his eyes to see the two blue-clad soldiers who were placing him on a stretcher.

137

"Stop your yelling, Reb," one of them said cheerfully. "You're not going to die—at least not today, anyway."

Nelson Majors gritted his teeth against the pain and looked around. All over the battlefield men were being gathered up and put into horse-drawn ambulances.

Looking down on him, the other soldier said, "Let me take a look at that side."

The lieutenant could not protest, and the other drew the shirt back. He whistled slightly. "Well, you'll have to see the surgeon for that. It's a good thing it didn't hit a little bit more in the front, or we'd be burying you instead of taking you to the hospital."

He tried to nod but the slightest action sent pain racing along his side. He gasped, "What—what's happening?"

The Union soldier frowned. "Well, it looks like you Rebs won this one. We got off the field, and they were still a-comin' at us. I guess we ought to leave you for them—but the lieutenant says take all the prisoners we can. There'll be one less of you to fight the next battle."

Lieutenant Majors felt unconsciousness coming back over him.

The soldiers carried him over to an ambulance wagon, where they placed him on the floor.

His last thought was, *I pray Tom and Jeff are all right . . .*

* * *

Tom and Jeff were all right but were nearly frantic at losing their father.

138

"We've got to go after him, Tom!" Jeff cried. "We can't let the Yankees have him!"

Tom shook his head. His face was black with powder, and he and Jeff were both trembling with fatigue. "We wouldn't get a mile, Jeff," he muttered. "The Yankees are retreating—but they'll get reinforcements right down the road."

Jeff looked around. "If they're retreating, why don't we chase them?"

Tom frowned. "That's just what Stonewall Jackson wanted to do—but the other officers wouldn't hear of it. They said we're too wore out and there's too many reinforcements in Washington." He sighed deeply. "I reckon they're right too. We're in no shape to be doing much chasing."

"Tom, I saw him go down, but I didn't get to see what happened after. He might be shot dead."

"Maybe not," Tom said grimly. "If not, he'll be exchanged."

"What does that mean?"

"It means we'll trade one of the captured Union officers we got to get him back."

"Do they do that?"

"Well, that's what I heard. Of course, there hasn't been no prisoners up till now," Tom said, "but now I know we got plenty of theirs." He waved at the lines of captured Union soldiers that were being herded away from the battle. He put his arm suddenly around Jeff's shoulders. "Come on, let's get something to eat. It's going to be a long march back to Richmond."

Tom looked over at the retreating Union line. "I wish we were going in to take Washington. I'd like to finish this thing once and for all. But it'll have to be another day."

He turned wearily away, and the two went back to join the lines that were forming for the trip back to Richmond. General Jackson came by on his horse, looking over the men and calling out encouraging words. Stopping beside Jeff and Tom, he said, "Your father was captured, I understand."

"Yes, sir. But we're believing he's all right— only wounded."

Jackson's eyes, which had been blazing with battle-madness, were now calm. He stroked his beard and held up his bandaged hand. "I pray that you're right. God will be with him and with all of you." He rode away, going from man to man.

Jeff watched him go, thinking, *I sure hope he'll help get my pa back!*

14

A Visitor for
the Lieutenant

The first spectators at the Battle of Bull Run returned to Washington about eight o'clock. Those who had left in mid-afternoon were convinced of a victory. However, by midnight the tumult and the dust and the terror of retreat had fallen upon the city. Rumors of defeat swept through the streets.

Finally President Abraham Lincoln received those who had watched the battle. He listened in silence as he heard of the rout. He did not go to bed all night.

Clouds whirled across the face of the moon as the Union army stumbled back across Long Bridge and Chain Bridge, scampering to Washington's safe, familiar streets. All night long they came in, most of them beaten, footsore, totally whipped. Occasionally a regiment marched in order, the men still bearing their arms with the look of soldiers.

Among them were some slightly wounded men, but more were lying strewn along the road from Fairfax Courthouse. A hospital was set up quickly in Alexandria, and the wounded were taken there in a steady stream.

MacDowell's army flooded into Washington. The troops stood in the wet streets around smoldering fires built from boards pulled from fences. Ladies stood in the rain handing out sandwiches and coffee. Citizens sent their carriages across the river to carry injured and exhausted men into town. The newspapers began at once to criticize the army for suffering such a defeat. A mob gathered in the streets, and soldiers were sent to bring order. Helplessly stretched in the mud, the capital awaited capture in the morning.

But no invasion came. Across Long Bridge came only the wagon trains, white-covered supply wagons, boxlike ambulances, country carts, and sutlers' vans. By noon Tuesday, Long Bridge was solidly blocked from end to end, and the cries of the wounded could be heard above the shouts of the drivers.

The North had not been prepared for defeat, and the military hospitals, small and understaffed, were soon overflowing.

Nelson Majors was one of a small group of Confederate officers that had been brought, first, to Alexandria. Finding the hospital full of Union officers, their guards took them on into Washington. Finally a place was set aside for them by order of General Scott's adjutant—an old warehouse, dark and dank.

There were no facilities and only a few beds. When Lieutenant Majors was brought in, he was placed on the rough blankets that had been wrapped around him on the battlefield. He lay on the hard floor, slowly becoming conscious of the sights and sounds around him.

"Where is this place?" he whispered to a Union soldier who had been set to guard the wounded prisoners.

"This is the old Capitol building, Reb," the soldier said. "For a while it was the Capitol of the whole United States, but it's been about everything else since then, including a prison. How you feeling?"

142

"I could use some water," Majors whispered.

"Well, it's against regulations, but you lie steady there, and I'll get you a drink."

Majors smiled as he thought of how useless the sentry's care was. *I couldn't run five steps—or even one, for that matter.*

Gratefully, he took the water the soldier brought, drank it, then handed the dipper back. "Thanks a lot, soldier. That was about the best drink I ever had."

He lay there quietly fighting against the pain, from time to time slipping into unconsciousness. Mostly he thought about Tom and Jeff. But he thought also of Royal and the other boys from Kentucky his son had grown up with who were now fighting on the Union side.

Finally a doctor came by, took one look at him, and said, "Get this man on a cot."

Hurriedly, a bed was obtained, and the lieutenant was placed on it by rough hands.

"Let me have a look at you, Lieutenant," the doctor said. He was an older man, fifty-five or sixty, with a shock of iron-gray hair and a pair of steady gray eyes. He was rough but efficient as he pulled back Nelson Majors's uniform and washed the wound. "That's a pretty bad wound you've got there. I'm going to have to probe for that ball, you understand?"

"Do what you need to, doctor. I appreciate the care."

His courtesy brought a sudden stare from the doctor. "I'm Dr. Cain. I have to tell you that your chances aren't very good." He pressed against the wound, bringing pain shooting through the lieutenant's side. "That ball probably took some of your uniform in with it. It's got a good chance of getting an infection, I'm afraid. But first I've got to get the ball out of there. Orderly . . ."

Jeff's father never liked to think about the operation, for although he was partly sedated it was a painful process. He awoke some time later, confused, and stared around. He had been brought into a room where there were six other cots, all occupied.

One man looked over at him and said, "Well, Lieutenant, you're still alive—and that's good."

He saw that the man wore the uniform of a captain and said, "I'm all right. How about you, Captain?"

"Oh, I'll be fine, except for this," he gestured down at his leg. His foot was missing.

"That's too bad, Captain."

"Aw, I'll get me a cork foot and be dancing the reel before you know it. My name is Steers," he said, "Burt Steers. Which outfit were you with?"

The two lay talking for a while. Finally, Jeff's father felt sleepy.

"You better get all the sleep you can," Steers said. "Anybody that goes through one of these operations needs lots of rest." He glanced around. "No need to worry. We're not going anywhere, and I'm not looking for any visitors. Are you?"

"No," the lieutenant said as he dropped off into a deep sleep. "No visitors . . . not for me."

* * *

"Well, you're doing better, Ira," Leah said with satisfaction. "As a matter of fact, it looks to me like you're able to get out of here."

It was two weeks after the Battle of Bull Run. Leah and her father had come regularly to visit Ira Pickens. His wound had given more trouble than he had expected, but now he looked fit. Leah sat beside him, asking how he had been.

He was sitting in a chair and had a cane that he used to walk with. She had brought him a cake that she had managed to bake, and he passed slices of it around to his companions, who devoured it eagerly.

One of them, a short, fat private from a New York regiment, grinned at Ira and gave him an obvious wink. "Wish I had a sweetheart to bring me cake like this. You got all the luck, Ira Pickens!"

Ira flushed. "Aw, it ain't all luck. I had to work at this, didn't I, Miss Leah?"

Leah was used to the men's teasing Ira about her being his girlfriend, and she did nothing to dissuade them. She sat there talking, telling Ira what was going on in Washington.

When she got up to leave, he said, "You know, one of the soldiers said they're keeping a bunch of Rebels next door. I reckon some of them are pretty bad off."

Leah stopped at once. "Next door? You mean that big old factory of a building?"

"That's it. The old Capitol. You can see it out the window here. Some of them get to walk around —with a guard, of course. Guess they're wishing they were back in the South."

"I hear they treated some of our fellows pretty rough, the Confederates did," a soldier growled. "I'd just as soon they all die."

Ira shook his head. "Don't talk like that, Slim. They mean well enough. They're just misled."

Leah stayed for only a short while longer, then went to her father. "You know there's a group of Rebel prisoners next to the hospital? The old Capitol building, they call it. I imagine they must be pretty lonely there. It'd be like being in jail, wouldn't it? And wounded too."

Her father looked at her carefully. "I expect you're right, Leah. I'll see what I can do about getting us a pass to go in. If you want to bake another one of your cakes, I'll get some Bibles and tracts."

"Do you think they'll let us go, Pa?"

"Well, I can't do anything but ask. But I don't see why not."

* * *

Lieutenant Nelson Majors had taken a turn for the worse. At first he seemed to be recovering from his operation, but, as the doctor had feared, some material from his uniform had been carried into the wound along with the bullet. The doctor had not been able to get it out. What started out as a simple fever turned out to be something much worse.

The doctor stopped by several times, and each time found this particular Confederate doing poorly. "Not much I can do for him," he informed the male nurse in charge of the Rebel prisoners. "Keep the wound cleaned out as best you can and try to get him to eat something. You know how these things go."

"Yes, Doctor. Three of them already died. I expect this lieutenant will be the fourth, if something doesn't happen."

Nelson Majors grew worse steadily so that at least half of the time he was in a strange coma—

146

not conscious or unconscious but somewhere in between. The pain in his side was somewhat less, but the high fever that gripped him most of the time seemed to burn him up. He continually was crying for water. No matter how much he drank, it was never enough.

He awakened early one morning feeling about as bad as he had ever felt in his entire life. His side was aflame with the infection, and he was burning with fever. The guards brought him something to eat, but he only drank the water.

He drifted off into a sleep of sorts and dreamed of Kentucky—of plowing the fields there, of hunting in the hills with the dogs. He dreamed of his wife and baby. Finally, he seemed to hear a voice calling him. He licked his lips and moved his head from side to side.

"Nelson, can you hear me?" the voice said.

The wounded man slowly opened his eyes, but when they focused he saw only the outline of two figures. Blinking, he whispered, "Can I have a drink of water?"

Almost at once a cup was at his lips and hands were holding him up. He drank thirstily. "Thanks," he said.

"Don't you know me, Nelson?"

The lieutenant was dizzy, and the man who spoke had his back to the light.

"No, I don't guess so," he whispered, and then he saw a young girl beside the man. At once he gasped, "Leah!" Then he looked up at the man, who turned so the light fell on his face. He reached up his hand, saying, "Dan Carter! What in the world . . ."

"Don't try to get up, Nelson," Leah's father said. "Me and Leah were sure surprised to see you.

We came to visit the Confederate wounded, and there you were."

"How long have you been here?"

"Oh, not too long." His old friend looked down at him and shook his head. "Sure sorry to see you here. If I'd known, we'd have been here a long time ago."

"No, we didn't even know there were Confederates here, Mr. Majors," Leah said quickly. "Are you badly hurt?"

"Bad enough, I guess. They pulled a bullet out of my side, and it hasn't done well."

His visitors looked at the bandage and back at his face.

"Are you getting enough to eat?" Leah asked.

"I'm not very hungry, not with this kind of fever."

She said, "Let me bathe your face with cool water. Maybe that will help."

Leah sought out the guard and apparently bullied him into giving her a basin of water and some cloths. She came back at once and began to bathe not only the lieutenant's face, but, pulling back the blanket, she bathed his body with the cool water.

"That's good," Nelson Majors whispered. He managed to smile. "You always were one for taking care of sick things—hurt animals. I remember that coon that got its paw cut off in a trap—how you and Jeff nursed him back to health."

"Do you remember that?" Leah said.

"Of course I do. You was always taking in some kind of stray critter." He looked down at himself and saw how much weight he had lost. "I guess that term really applies to me—a stray critter."

"Are Jeff and Tom all right?" Leah asked, continuing to bathe his heated flesh.

A troubled look came into Nelson Majors's eyes. "I can't find out anything. I've been too sick to move." Eagerly he looked up. "Maybe you could find out for me, Leah. Could you write for me?"

"Why, I'll do that," Leah said quickly. "When was the last time you saw them?"

"It was in the battle. They were all right when I left, but I got ahead and then got cut off. Then I got hit and don't remember much after that."

"Don't worry," Leah said. "Now that I know you're here, I'll be in every day. I'll bring you something good to eat, and you'll be well soon. You'll see!"

* * *

Leah was as good as her word. For the next week, she was at the prison hospital every day. At first the administrator, a young major, was reluctant to admit her, but finally she wore his resistance down, and he threw up his hands. "Well, all right. Go ahead and do what you can for him. We'll have to make sure you don't let any of them escape."

Leah smiled up at him. "Thank you, Major. God bless you for your kindness."

This brought a flush to the young man's face, and he seemed not to know how to answer her.

At once Leah wrote a letter to Nelson Majors's commanding officer and posted it. However, she had been told that the mails were slow, especially those crossing the enemy lines, and she warned Jeff's father not to expect a quick reply.

"I just pray that they're all right," he said. He smiled as, sitting in the chair beside him, she fed him the broth that she had brought. "I bet you never thought you'd have me for a patient, did you, Leah?"

"I'm glad that I'm here to help." When she finished, she sat back and began to speak of Esther. "She's a darling child, Mr. Majors," she said. "One of the prettiest babies I've ever seen. And such a good baby too."

"I don't know what I would have done if it hadn't been for you and your family, Leah." He gave her another look. "It's a good thing you and Jeff are such good friends, or I never would have had that kind of help."

Two days later, Leah came in, her face beaming. "I have a letter from home," she said. "Esther is fine. Let me read it to you."

She read aloud the letter from her mother, and when she had finished she said, "Now you see the baby is fine, and I know that Tom and Jeff are going to be fine too."

Nelson Majors had lain quietly listening to the news. "I wonder if I'll ever be able to be a father to Esther. It'll be hard with this war on."

"It'll be all right. The war will end, and you'll have Esther back again—and Jeff and Tom too."

He looked at her fondly. "You're a fine girl, Leah. I thank God for you and the help you've been to me." Then he smiled and said, "I guess you Carters get pretty tired of taking care of us Majorses, don't you?"

Leah looked up. "No," she said quickly, "we never get tired of that."

"You're growing up real fast. It seems only a week or two ago that you and Jeff were just small children playing under the wagon. Those were good days, weren't they?"

"Yes, they were," Leah whispered. Then she leaned forward and patted his arm. "And they'll come again—don't you worry about it. Jeff and I may be too old to play under a wagon, but we'll be together again, and you'll be with Esther, and maybe some day Tom and Sarah will be together too."

"I'm glad you feel like that—always thinking things will end right. I hope you always do, Leah," Lieutenant Majors said. Then weariness seemed to come upon him, he closed his eyes, and he dropped off to sleep.

Leah arranged the blanket around him, then sat back thinking of those days when she and Jeff had played under a wagon and gone hunting for birds' eggs—and the thousand-and-one times they had wandered through the hills together.

"I wish it were now," she whispered. "I wish that Jeff and I could do those things right now!"

15

General
Stonewall Jackson

The victory of Bull Run—or Manassas, as people from the North called it—proved to be the greatest misfortune that could have befallen the Confederacy.

The victory was taken by the Southern public as the end of the war—or at least its decisive event. This conviction was not only held by the man in the street, but after the battle even President Jefferson Davis assured his friends that the recognition of the Confederate states by the European countries was now certain. The newspapers declared that the question of manhood between North and South was settled forever, and the phrase "One Southerner equal to five Yankees" was used in all speeches about the war—although sometimes the rule moved up to one Southerner to seven Yankees.

On the whole, the unfortunate victory was followed by a period of fancied security and relaxed exertion. The best proof of this was to be found in the decrease of enlistments by volunteers. Then there actually arose a controversy between different Southern states as to the location of the capital of the government—which was strange, considering its existence was in peril.

Stonewall Jackson echoed the sentiments of a few wise leaders in the South when he said, "It would have been better if we had lost at Bull Run.

Our people have been lulled into a sense of false security, and when the Yankees come back with the enormous army they are bound to raise, all of us will soon know the truth of what a hard war this will be."

The North, although bitterly disappointed by the outcome of the battle, did not fold up and quit as Southerners expected. They gritted their teeth, settled down for a long war, and moved toward producing a war machine the like of which the world had never seen.

The leadership of the North's military was in confusion, however. Those who commanded at Bull Run, especially General MacDowell, were considered ineffective, and President Lincoln began to search for a new commanding officer.

The soldiers themselves presented a rather gloomy front. Some of them were ready to go home, and one officer came to General Sherman and announced, "General, I'm going to take my group back to New York today."

Sherman said, "I don't remember signing a leave for you."

When the officer argued with him, General Sherman said sharply, "Captain, if you attempt to leave without orders, I will shoot you like a dog!"

Later that same day, President Lincoln arrived. After he had addressed the troops, the officer who had attempted to leave forced his way to the president's carriage. "Mr. President, I have a cause of grievance. This morning I went to General Sherman, and he threatened to shoot me."

Mr. Lincoln looked at him and then at Sherman. Stooping his tall, spare form toward the officer, he said to him in a loud stage whisper, "Well, if I were

you, and General Sherman threatened to shoot me
—I would not trust him—I believe he would do it!"

Finally recognizing that the war against the
Confederacy would not be a walk-over, Lincoln cast
around for the right man to put the army together.
He chose George B. McClellan, only thirty-four years
of age, former president of the Ohio and Mississippi
Railroad. McClellan proved to be an excellent or-
ganizational man, and soon the Army of the Potomac
began to swell with new volunteers and rapidly became a powerful weapon for the North.

In the South, the Confederate administration
strove to bring order out of chaos. The Tredegar
Works in Richmond glowed all night. Its tall chim-
neys belched out dense, luminous smoke. Huge
trainloads of heavy guns and improved ordnance
of every kind were shipped off to points threatened
by the Federal troops.

The medical department, destined to play so
important and needful a part in the coming days,
was thoroughly reorganized. Surgeons of all ages,
some of them with the highest reputation in the
South, left their homes to take service with the
army.

The Confederate soldiers knew the odds they
confronted numerically. And they not only had to
face overwhelming numbers, but the arms and the
ammunition of the Federal soldiers were abundant
and good.

The Confederate soldiers were deprived of chlo-
roform and morphine—these were excluded from
the Confederacy as contraband of war. Then, some
actually opposed certain improvements that their
government tried to bring about, such as a sanitary
commission and even the newly equipped ambu-

lances. They got few of these, while the Federals got many.

But of all this Jeff and Tom were only vaguely aware. After Bull Run, the Stonewall Brigade rapidly filled the gaps in its ranks with volunteers. The time would come when men would have to be drafted into the service, but at this point there was still enough excitement and glamour to the war to entice young men from all over the South to join up. The Stonewall Brigade easily was the most famous in the entire Confederate army. Stonewall's gallant performance at the Battle of Bull Run had made his name a household word.

But if General Jackson was a famous man, he was also a hard-driving man. He pushed his troops into a training program that left them exhausted. Almost every day he led them on forced marches and again earned them the name of Jackson's Foot Cavalry.

At first, Jeff nearly collapsed under the strain of the long marches. Many of the men did, simply walking themselves into the ground and falling to one side. Strangely enough, Jackson, who was a compassionate man in almost every other respect, seemed to have little thought for such men. He was a hard general, and one of his officers said, "I tremble every time General Jackson comes up. I always half expect him to give me an order to storm the North Pole!"

Slowly, however, as time passed after Bull Run, the army toughened up.

Jeff and Tom stayed very close together, waiting anxiously for word to come from their father. One day after retreat had been sounded and the two were seated before a campfire, staring into it and saying little, Jeff broke the silence.

"Tom," he said in a low voice, "I can't help but think that—well, maybe Pa got killed."

Tom shoved his forage cap back on his head, leaned back, and stared across the fire. The flickering yellow flames cast shadows on Jeff's face, making it look angular and very young. "You don't know that, Jeff. Lots of our men were wounded and got taken prisoner by the Yankees."

"Why doesn't he write us then?" Jeff argued. "If he's alive, he must know that we're worried about him."

"Can't answer that." Tom picked up his bayonet and poked at the fire, sending a myriad sparks whirling into the upper air. He watched them until they faded out, then said, "He may be hurt too bad to write—and I don't reckon the Yankees will be pampering our fellows too much."

Tom suddenly felt tired and depressed. He knew that it was up to him to cheer his younger brother. However, he himself had had thoughts such as Jeff expressed. Nonetheless, he said as cheerfully as possible, "I think they would have told us if he had died. I just have to believe he's wounded and not able to get a letter to us. It's not easy to get a letter across the lines—no regular mail service, you know."

A soldier named Jed Hawkins, a member of their squad, was sitting back from the fire. He was a fine musician and carried his guitar everywhere he could, except into battle. He would have carried it there, but the sergeant had sternly ordered him to leave it in the rear. "You can't kill a Yankee with a guitar," Sergeant Mapes said angrily. Then he added, "You play the thing so bad, that might hurt some of them a little bit. But leave that blasted thing behind."

Jed began fingering the guitar, sending tinkling, melodious sounds over the night air. As the rest of the squad sat exhausted after their hard day's march, he lifted his voice and began to sing. He sang a song called "Lorena," a favorite with both Yankees and Rebels. The words were sad, and Hawkins's fine tenor voice fell on the summer air:

"The years creep slowly by, Lorena,
  The snow is on the grass again;
  The sun's low down the sky, Lorena,
  The frost gleams where the flowers have been.

"But the heart throbs warmly now,
  As when the summer days were nigh;
  Oh, the sun can never dip so low,
  Adown affection's cloudless sky."

Tom gave a disparaging look toward the singer. "Don't you know any cheerful songs, Jed? All you do is sing those miserable, sad things!"

Hawkins, a small, lean man with black hair and dark eyes, grinned. "Sure I do. How about this one:

"There's a spot that the soldiers all love,
  The mess tent's the place that we mean,
  And the dish we best like to see there
  Is the old-fashioned white army bean!

"Now the bean in its primitive state
  Is a plant we have all often met,
  And when cooked in the old army style
  It has charms we can never forget!

"'Tis the bean that we mean,
And we'll eat as we ne'er ate before;
The army bean, nice and clean—
We'll stick to our beans evermore!"

The song had barely ended when Sergeant Mapes said, "You fellows better pile in. You're going to be going on another little pleasure walk tomorrow."

A groan went up.

One of the men said, "Don't Old Blue Light ever take a rest? All he wants to do is hear preaching and kill us on forced marches!"

Jeff privately agreed but didn't say much. Finally he got up. "I hope we hear from Pa soon, Tom. It's going to drive me crazy if we don't." He left his brother with the squad and found Charlie Bowers already in their small tent.

"Hey, Jeff," Bowers said. "You better get on to sleep. I heard we're going on another march tomorrow."

When Jeff only grunted and finally settled himself down on his blankets beside the smaller boy, Charlie asked tentatively, "I guess you didn't hear nothing about your Pa yet, huh?"

"Not yet."

Charlie studied the brief answer. "Well, I'm going to pray that he's all right. I've been doing that anyhow."

Jeff lifted his head, placed it on his palm, and stared at the dim figure beside him. "You really think praying does any good? My ma always said that it did—but I've asked for a few things, and sometimes I got 'em, and sometimes I didn't."

"Why, sure it does good!" Bowers seemed astonished at the question. "You ought to know better than that, Jeff. The Bible says we have to ask and we'll receive."

Jeff lay down in the darkness, thinking about what Charlie had said. The last thing he did before drifting off to sleep was to make a vow. *Well, I don't know if prayer does any good or not, but I've tried everything else, so I'll try that.*

He hesitated, then said, *God, I don't know how to pray except just to say I sure would appreciate it if You would take care of Pa. He may be beyond help, but if Ma and people like Charlie are right, then You're able to do anything. So I'm asking You to take care of Pa and keep him safe.*

A bugle sounded a sad tune far off in the distance, and then Jeff wearily closed his eyes and went to sleep.

* * *

When Jeff awakened the next morning, the first thing he thought was, *Well, I've done the praying; now let's see if God will come through.* At once he was ashamed and shook his head. *Can't think about God like that!*

As the sergeant had promised, they made a hard march that day. When they got back, Jeff was so tired he barely had enough strength to go down and wash off at the creek. Then he joined his squad in the supper they had thrown together. Though it was only hardtack and biscuit, he gobbled down his share.

Charlie Bowers came over to say, "Jeff, General Jackson's asked everybody to come to a special service tonight. Let's go over and hear the preaching."

"Aw, I'm too tired," Jeff protested. But as Charlie attempted to persuade him, he finally said, "Well, if I'm going to learn how to pray, I guess that'd be a good place to do it." He nodded reluctantly. "All right, Charlie. I'm wore out and will probably go to sleep during the sermon, but I'll go with you."

They made their way over to the parade ground where they found hundreds of men already seated on the grass. There was a platform where the chaplain would stand. It was lit by two bonfires on each side.

"Look, there's General Lee. See him standing right beside our general?" Charlie Bowers whispered. "He sure is a fine-looking man, ain't he?"

The two boys sat down, and soon the singing began. After that, the chaplain preached. Jeff was so tired he could hardly sit up. Several times his head nodded, and he came to with a snap. Looking around, however, he saw that he wasn't the only tired one.

Finally the sermon was over, and, as he expected, some of the soldiers went forward when the chaplain invited them.

A thought came to Jeff. He said, "Charlie, I'm going to go talk to General Jackson. This may be the only chance I'll get."

"About getting saved, you mean?"

"No, about my pa. You wait here, Charlie, or go on back to the camp."

"I'll wait," Charlie said. "You go on and see the general."

Jeff moved through the men, noticing that some of them were on their knees and had their eyes closed. Then he stood off on one side, close enough to see General Jackson go to one, then another, putting his hand on their shoulders at times, leaning over to whisper to them.

Jeff thought, *He sure is different than on the battlefield. He's a wild man out there, and now, why, he's just as gentle as any woman I ever saw!*

He waited patiently until the last soldier had left, then he went to the general and said, uncertainly, "General Jackson . . . uh . . . could I speak to you, sir?"

Jackson turned. "Why, it's young Majors, isn't it?"

"Yes, sir." Jeff hesitated, then said, "I know you're real busy, General, but I came to ask you to do me a favor."

"What is it, my boy?"

"Well, Pa was captured after Bull Run, you know?"

Jackson nodded. Compassion was on his long face. "I know. I miss him greatly. But not as much as you do, of course. What is it you want me to do, my boy?"

Jeff said, "Well, last night I did something I haven't done much of. My ma, she was a praying woman, but she's dead. And I didn't know anything to do, so last night I prayed that God would take care of my pa."

Jackson's face lit up. "Why, that's exactly what you should have done, Jeff."

"Well, there's one more thing. I thought maybe you would see about getting my pa exchanged. I hear that we'll swap some of the Yankee officers we took for some they took. So I was wondering if you couldn't let my pa be one of those."

Jackson studied the boy's face. "Do you know the Lord, Jeff?"

Jeff was an honest young man. He shook his head. "No, sir, not very good. My ma did, though, and so does Pa, and my brother, Tom, too, I reckon."

"Well," Jackson said, "it would be easier for you to pray if you could go to God as a loving Father." He talked with Jeff about becoming a Christian, until the boy felt nervous. He finally said, "Well, I will do what I can, but you must have faith in God."

Jeff blurted out without thinking, "I've got faith in Stonewall Jackson!"

Jackson laughed but then shook his head. "'Put not your trust in princes,'" he admonished. "The Bible says that. However, I will do what I can to see about getting your father exchanged."

Jeff beamed. "Thank you, General Jackson." Then he turned and left.

When he found Charlie waiting, he said, "Well, I talked to the general, and he's going to try and get Pa exchanged."

"I told you prayer would work."

Jeff looked after General Jackson, who was disappearing into the darkness with his staff. "I don't know," he said doubtfully. "I've got a lot of faith in General Jackson, but I don't guess I'll believe it until I actually see my pa set free from the Yankees!"

16
Back to Kentucky

Tom! Tom! Look what I got!"

Tom Majors looked up from the musket he was cleaning and, seeing joy on his brother's face, leaped to his feet. "Is it a letter from Pa?"

"Yes, I think so," Jeff said. "It just came. Look, it's addressed to both of us." He held up the envelope.

Tom stared at it and frowned. "I don't know that handwriting. It's not Pa's, though."

"No, it's Leah's." Jeff was almost jumping up and down with excitement. "I didn't open it because I wanted us to read it together."

"Well, open it now," Tom said quickly. He watched nervously as Jeff tore open the envelope and then moved to stand beside him. "You read it aloud, Jeff, while I look over your shoulder."

"All right." And Jeff began to read:

Dear Jeff and Tom,

You will be surprised to hear from me, but you will be glad when you hear the news. Your father is well! He's a prisoner in a hospital in Washington. My father and I were visiting the Confederate prisoners there, and I couldn't believe it when we found him.

That's the good news, but I'm afraid he is still suffering greatly from the wound he received. It got infected, and for some time he had a serious, real high fever. Father and I came to see him every day and did what we could to make things better for him. He didn't have any appetite at first, but he is doing better now, and the fever seems to be going down.

I don't have time to write any more because I want to get this in the mail. I know both of you are worried about him, and he says to give you his love and that he will write you a letter himself, and I will mail it for him. Try not to worry too much about him. Pa and I will take care of him as best we can. Pa and I have been worried about both of you, and I hope that neither one of you was injured in the battle.

I received a letter from home just yesterday, and Esther is fine and healthy. We will be leaving here shortly to make a trip home, and I will write you from there.

Your friend,
Leah Carter

Jeff looked up, and relief washed across his face. "Boy, that's a relief, isn't it, Tom?"

"It sure is." Tom pulled out a handkerchief and wiped his forehead. "I couldn't help worrying and wondering, and it's great to hear that he's all right."

Jeff looked at the letter again. "But it doesn't sound like he's doing too well, does it?"

"No, he would have been all right by now if it had been a simple wound." Tom's brow furrowed. "We've got to get him out of that hospital somehow. Did General Jackson say anything to you? You seem to have an inside track with him."

"No, I only talked to him once, and he said that he had turned Pa's name over to the commission that takes care of prisoner exchanges. He said he recommended that one of the Yankees be exchanged for Pa as soon as possible."

Tom nodded eagerly. "It's a good thing you went to him, Jeff. I would never have thought of going to a general and asking a favor like that."

"Well, I hope the job gets done. But you know the general warned me that they'd be more likely to exchange one of the Union prisoners for a healthy man. We need all the active soldiers we can get. Of course, with General Jackson's name on it, that ought to mean something."

"I think it will, and we'll just have to pray that it'll go through and that Pa will be back with us soon."

* * *

By the end of August both Tom and Jeff had lost hope of an early exchange for their father. They went about their duties, and the army seemed to have settled down into a routine.

However, one day Tom found Jeff while he was practicing on his drum. He looked excited. "Jeff, I've got some good news—at least I think it is."

Jeff put down the drum. "What is it, Tom—something about Pa?"

"Well, not exactly. Captain Brandon told me about a herd of horses that were to be had over in Kentucky—in Boone County. He wants me to take a few men and go bring them back."

"Why, that's the county next to ours," Jeff said. His face lit up. "You're taking *me*, aren't you, Tom?"

"Why, who else would I take? There'll be a pretty good herd, so the Captain said to choose three men, and you're one of them. Get your stuff together, because we're going to leave right away."

"Will we have time to go by home?"

"Sure, it's right on the way." Tom grinned suddenly. "This way we'll have a chance to see our baby sister. Get yourself ready now. We'll be leaving in a couple of hours."

Jeff gave him a fond look. "I wish we could just go on to Washington and get Pa out of that prison hospital."

"Well, we can't, but at least we can go see how Esther is doing," Tom said and then left quickly.

* * *

"I declare, you two certainly look fine!" Mrs. Carter met the boys as they came into the yard and dismounted.

They had sent on the other two soldiers to begin gathering the horses and took a shortcut to the Carter household.

Jeff looked around anxiously. "The place looks just the same, Mrs. Carter. It sure is good to see it again and you too."

Sarah came out to stand beside her mother. She was wearing a light blue dress that went with her dark blue eyes, and Tom could not take his eyes off her.

"I'm glad to see you, Tom—and you too, Jeff," she said quietly. "I guess I'm surprised to see you in civilian clothes, although I should have known better."

"No, it wouldn't be very smart to wear our uniforms here in Kentucky. I guess it's still kind of a no-man's land here, isn't it?"

"Yes, it is, Tom," Mrs. Carter said. "Our people still are divided, so it's better you just wear what you've got on." Then she said, "Come on in now and see that fat, old baby sister of yours."

Eagerly the two young men went into the house.

Mrs. Carter went over to a cradle and picked up the baby, who began screaming at the top of her lungs.

"Here," she said, thrusting the squalling infant on Tom. "She's glad to see you. That's why she cries so hard."

"I'd hate to hear how much she hollered if she wasn't glad to see me." He held the baby awkwardly and looked down at her.

Suddenly Esther stopped crying and looked up at the face above hers. Her eyes were very blue, and her hair was fine and blonde.

"Why, she looks like Ma," Tom murmured and put his finger out to touch her soft cheek. "I don't know much about babies, but this one seems especially fine to me."

"She is! She's the most beautiful baby in the world," Sarah said.

Morena, who had been standing to one side, joined them.

When Jeff spoke to her, saying, "Hello, Morena," she gave him a bright smile.

"Morena loves the baby," Sarah said. "She will sit and hold her for hours. She'll have that child spoiled to death."

"Here, let me hold her, Tom," Jeff said. "I have more experience than you have." He took the baby, held her so that he could see her face, and then smiled down at her. "You and me—we've already done some traveling together, haven't we, baby sister?"

"You come in," Sarah said. "We'll have something fixed for you to eat in no time."

"That sounds good to me, Sarah." Tom smiled at her. "I think I could eat a hawk."

"Well, we don't have any of those, but we do have a chicken ready to fry and some sweet potatoes like you always liked."

"Oh," Tom groaned. "Don't talk about it! I've eaten so many beans and hardtack, I believe I've lost my taster."

"I doubt that."

Sarah was obviously very glad to see Tom, and all during the meal she kept her eyes on him as if she couldn't bear to look at anything else.

As they ate, Jeff did most of the talking. "I don't know what we'd a-done if it hadn't been for Leah and your husband, Mrs. Carter," he said. He stuffed his mouth full of sweet potato, swallowed, and started to talk again.

But Mrs. Carter interrupted him. "I declare, Jeff Majors. I don't think you ever taste anything. You shove your food back and swallow it in one gulp like a snake or something. Eat slowly—you'll enjoy it better."

Jeff grinned, unabashed. "I can't help it! This food is so good after what we've been eating. I just want to gobble it down like a bluetick hound."

"Well, there's plenty of it, and you'll have time to eat all you want," she said. "How long can you stay?"

"It'll take two or three days to gather the herd together," Tom said. He glanced at Sarah. "I hope we get to spend most of it here, though we'll have to help the other fellows collect the horses."

"We've got plenty of room now. You can sleep in the attic room upstairs."

"Did you know that Leah and her father are on their way back from Washington?" Mrs. Carter asked.

"I didn't know when," Jeff answered, "but she said in her letter they were coming back. I sure hope they come before we leave. I'd like to see them both again."

"And you and Leah will go out hunting birds' eggs, I expect." Sarah laughed. "You ought to have enough birds' eggs collected to fill this house."

Jeff was a little embarrassed at the reference to the hobby he and Leah had developed, but he grinned. "That'd be more fun that having our legs walked off by Stonewall Jackson."

The two sat and enjoyed their meal.

That afternoon Jeff and Tom walked over to their old home place and visited with the family that had bought it.

"It makes me a little homesick," Jeff said as he and Tom came back to the Carter house, "seeing strangers living in our house."

"It's not our house anymore. Virginia's our home now. I guess it always will be."

His words depressed Jeff. He decided to go off to fish in the creek.

* * *

Tom looked for Sarah. "Come for a walk with me?"

"Shall we bring your sister along?"

He saw the mischievous look in her eyes and shook his head, "No, I have to get used to having a baby in the family. Right now I just want to stretch my legs. That was a long ride, all the way from Richmond."

They left the house and walked along the pathways Tom knew so well. They crossed the creek, then followed its winding down to the woods. It was quiet there. Only the trickling of water over stones and the soft crying of birds was heard as they made their way through the forest.

Once there was a scurrying in the brush ahead of them, and Tom reached out to take Sarah's arm. "Wait a minute," he whispered.

They stood and watched as a very young deer stepped nervously from behind a thicket. He seemed to be searching the forest, and Tom knew that as long as they stayed absolutely still, he would probably not see them. Then, with a startled snort, he bounded into the air and disappeared into the woods.

"Beautiful," Tom said. Then a thought came to him, and he grinned. "He'd better not get around that camp of ours. He'd find himself roasting over a fire somewhere."

Sarah sat on a fallen log. She looked up at him, and the sun flickering through the green foliage overhead fell on her with an amber light. Her dark hair and dark blue eyes were beautiful. He studied her oval face, noting again the beautiful creamy complexion.

"Was it very bad?" she asked gently. "The fighting?"

"Yes, terrible," Tom said frankly. He sat down beside her, picked up a stick, and began to draw a pattern on the ground. "I thought I knew what to expect, but it wasn't anything like that." He began to tell her a little of the horrors of battle, of the men that fell like bundles, the screaming of the wounded, the crying out for water. Finally, he tossed the stick away and turned to face her. "It's the most terrible thing in the world, war. I wish I didn't have to go back to it."

Sarah reached out and took his hand.

She was not a demonstrative girl, and this surprised him. But her eyes were intent as she whispered, "I wish you didn't have to go back at all, Tom. I wish there wasn't any war, and things were back like they were when we were younger."

"That was a simple time, wasn't it?" He was very conscious of her hand on his, and he caught the scent of violets, which she always wore. Without thinking he reached over and pulled her forward.

It was a natural thing to do to kiss her on the lips, and she clung to him for a moment.

"Oh, Tom," she whispered, "will we ever be able to have each other like we've always planned?"

"One day." He held her close and ran his hand down her silky black hair, the blackest hair possible, and then held her out at arms' length. "One day," he said, "it'll be over. Then we can get married."

She bit her lip, and he saw that she was not far from tears. "I try to think like that, Tom. Then I think about Royal and about you and your father and Jeff, about thousands and thousands of young

171

men just like you. And sometimes it seems like there's no hope."

He pulled her close again and held her. The quiet ran on for a long time. Finally, he drew back and sighed. "Some day it'll be different. But until then, we'll just do what we have to do."

Sarah brushed her eyes with her hands. "Come on," she said, "let's go back to the house. I'm going to make one of those squash casseroles you like so well—and anything else you want to eat."

"That's the way I like to hear you talk." Tom grinned. The moment had passed, but as they returned to the house he knew that there was a sadness in him that was tied up with the doubts that the war had brought. *It'll be a long, long time before I can have this girl,* he thought. *A thousand things could happen. I could get killed or even wounded so badly I couldn't ask her to marry me.*

When he saw Jeff sitting on the front steps playing with Esther, he breathed a little prayer. *Lord, you've brought us this far, now take us the rest of the way.*

17

We Just Have
to Believe God

J eff, I can't believe you're really here."

Jeff grinned self-consciously as Leah came up
to him. He thought for a moment that she meant to
throw her arms around him. Then she must have
seen her parents smiling—and Tom and Sarah as
well.

Awkwardly he put out his hand. "Why, it's good
to see you again, Leah!"

Leah took the hand he held out and held on to
it. Her eyes were on his face. "You're so brown!"
she exclaimed. "And I declare, I believe you've
grown taller! Isn't he taller, Pa?"

"I think he is, Pet." Her father smiled. He looked
tired, for the trip had been wearing—but he was
obviously glad to see the two boys. "Let me get
some of this dust knocked off of me, then I'll tell
you about your pa."

His wife led him off, asking about his trip, and
Leah looked down at herself. She was wearing a
pair of faded overalls, which would have been very
comfortable on the trail, but now she seemed embarrassed to be dressed in such old clothes. She
said, "Let me go wash up too, Jeff." She could not
resist squeezing his arm and saying, "I'm so glad
you're here!"

She ran lightly away, and as her footsteps echoed on the stairs, Jeff gave another self-conscious look toward Tom and Sarah.

"Well, what are you two laughing about?" he demanded, his face growing rosy. "I don't see anything funny."

Sarah took pity on him. "We're just happy to see Pa and Leah," she said quickly.

Tom, taking the hint, agreed. "Yes, that's it. It's good to see them both."

Thirty minutes later the men were all sitting at the table preparing to eat the meal that Mrs. Carter had put together—baked ham, potato salad, cornbread, fresh onions, and two loaves of freshly baked bread.

When the food was on the table, she went to the landing and called up, "Leah, get yourself down here. These men are starving to death."

"That girl's going to be late for the resurrection," her father said, but he smiled. "I don't think I could've made it without her. She's got enough energy for any two girls I ever saw." He continued to talk about how well Leah had done as they followed the troops. At the sound of her footsteps in the foyer, he looked up and urged, "Come on in, daughter—" and then he stopped abruptly.

Everyone turned to look and discovered that the dusty girl in overalls had disappeared.

"Well," Tom said, "who is this young lady? I don't believe I've ever met her before." He winked at Sarah, who smiled back.

Leah had put on her best dress, something she usually wore only as Sunday-go-to-meeting clothes. She wore a deep green, cotton sateen dress with bands of satin ribbon stitched into place with white silk thread. A pair of fine black shoes that she had been saving for a special occasion peeked out from under her skirt. Her fine, blonde hair was parted in the middle, and the curls were pulled to the side from the center part. They curled in front of her ears, giving her a rather saucy look. The hairstyle made her eyes seem larger, and it appeared she had borrowed some of Sarah's rice powder for her face.

Now that she was the target of every eye, she suddenly blushed. "Well, I don't know what you're all staring at! Can't a girl get dressed up every once in a while?"

Tom grinned at her. "You look fine, Leah, just fine." He couldn't resist adding, "If you drop dead, we won't have to do a thing to you except stick a lily in your hand."

"Tom, what an awful thing to say!" Sarah admonished him but could not restrain a giggle. "Come on in, Leah. I don't believe I've ever seen you look so pretty."

Leah took the seat across from Jeff, who was staring at her with wide-open eyes.

"Shoot," he muttered, "you make me feel like a tramp, Leah. I didn't know we were supposed to get dressed up just to eat dinner."

"Stop picking on her, Jeff," her mother said. "After weeks of traipsing all over the country wearing those old overalls, I don't wonder that she wants to dress up. You look beautiful, dear. Now, ask the blessing, Dan, and make it a short one—everyone's hungry."

He looked up at her with a smile. "I'll be as brief as possible, but I must give thanks for having these special guests with us."

He prayed, and then they all plunged in. As they ate, Dan Carter, who ate little himself, reviewed what had happened to the boys' father. He did not try to lessen the seriousness of his illness. "He really ought to be in a regular hospital. I'm afraid that the authorities give the Northern boys the best of things, and the prisoners have to take what's left over."

Tom said sharply, "That's not right—" Then he paused and shrugged his shoulders wearily. "But I guess it's probably the same in the South."

Jeff said, "How did he look when you left?"

Leah and her father exchanged a quick look.

She said, "He was better than when we first saw him, Jeff. But they're going to transfer him to the old Capitol Prison."

Jeff caught something in her voice, glanced over at Tom, and then back at Leah. "What's the old Capitol Prison?"

"It's an old building that they're using for a penitentiary now. We heard they're going to put the Confederate officers in part of it," Mr. Carter said.

"What's it like?" Tom demanded.

Dan described the poor conditions, and finally Leah said, "But we'll be going back, and we'll be able to visit him regularly. We'll see that he gets good food and blankets and things like that."

Tom shook his head, and Jeff knew his brother's dissatisfaction was mirrored on his own face. "I wish we could go be with him."

"You wouldn't last long in that place," Dan Carter said sharply. "They've got secret agents out looking for Confederate spies. You'd get picked up in two days."

Jeff said, "They wouldn't be looking for a boy. I don't see why I couldn't go."

"You're in the army, Jeff," Tom reminded him. "We've both got to be going as soon as we get the horses together."

Little more was said, but all that day Jeff was very quiet.

Leah noticed that he was not cheerful, and late that afternoon she said, "Jeff, let's go down and try to catch old Napoleon." She had changed the fancy dress for a simple blue one.

Jeff did not feel like fishing, but at her urging they dug some worms, grabbed the poles, and made their way down to the river. It was growing late when they got there. The sun was red in the sky and cast red reflections on the water.

"Too hot to fish much," Jeff said idly, "but I guess we might as well try." They baited their hooks and found a deep pool where they had seen old Napoleon many times.

As they fished, Leah tried to be cheerful, but she could tell that Jeff was depressed. She said, "It's been hard on you and Tom, hasn't it?"

Jeff nodded. He looked miserable, and his face was drawn. "I worry about Pa," he said quietly. "If there was only something I could do for him!"

Leah put her hand on his forearm. "We'll do all we can, Jeff."

He managed to smile. "I know you will, Leah. You've been swell. You've been great to take care of Pa the way you have. I just don't know how to thank you—"

Suddenly Jeff's cork disappeared with a loud *plop!* He let out a yell. "It's a big 'un!" He heaved back on the pole and set the hook, but the line zig-zagged frantically across the water. He held on.

Leah knew that if he gave any slack, he would lose the fish. "I wish we had a net!" he shouted. "I don't think we can land one this big! He'll flop off."

"You can do it, Jeff!" Leah threw down her pole and watched with excitement.

Jeff fought, but the fish pulled so hard that she was afraid the pole or the line would break. Finally, however, he brought the fish to the surface and as soon as he did he yelled, "It's him! It's old Napoleon!"

"I'll get him, Jeff. Pull him in! Pull him in!" Leah screamed. She waded out into the water, and when Jeff worked the fish ashore she put her thumb inside the huge fish's mouth and clamped down on it.

"I've got him!" She squealed and turned to move to shore. But then she stepped in a hole and fell splashing into the water.

"Don't let him go!" Jeff cried. He sloshed over, put one arm around her, and pulled her to her feet, still holding the fish. He picked her up and carried her ashore saying, "You hold onto the fish, and I'll hold onto you."

"All right," Leah said, "but hurry up! He's so heavy!"

Jeff carried her ten feet away from the bank, put her down, then reached out carefully and took the fish. The huge bass flopped frantically as he removed the hook, then seemed to give up.

Jeff stood watching as the red beams of the sun played over the beautiful scales of the fish. Then he gave Leah an odd look. Without a word he turned and walked back to the river. Leaning over, he slowly put the fish into the water and released him.

There was a powerful splash and the silver glint of scales as Napoleon disappeared into the reeds that lined the bank.

Leah walked up and stood beside him. "You let him go, Jeff?" Her voice was a whisper, and when he didn't answer she pulled on his arm until he turned around. "Why did you do that?"

"I don't know. He put up such a good fight. And somehow I want to think about Napoleon being in this river. Maybe when the war is over I'll come back and have another chance at him. I've thought about him so often. I just want him to be here." Then he said suddenly, "I'm going to see my father, Leah."

She gasped. "But, Jeff—you can't!"

"I'm going to see him," he said stubbornly, "and that's all there is to it."

"But if you get caught they might hang you for a spy!"

"They can't hang me but once, can they?" He found a smile. "I don't know if I'm an actor or not—but I'm sure going to act like a good Yankee just come to visit the soldiers in prison."

Leah looked up at him. My, he did seem taller. She looked down at her dress, which was soaked and clung to her. Then she looked up again. Her lips were soft, and her eyes were filled with a strange affection. She said, "Well, if you go, I'm going with you. They'd spot a Rebel like you a mile off!"

"Why—you can't do that!" Jeff argued. "You stay away from me. If I get caught I don't want you caught too."

Leah's eyes flashed. "I can be just as stubborn as you can be, Jeff Majors, and we're going to do this thing together." She thought a moment. "Maybe we can pretend to be brother and sister—that'd be a good thing, wouldn't it?"

"Yeah," Jeff said, wonder coming into his voice. "That would help, wouldn't it?" He grinned at her and said, "I've never had a sister like you. Just a baby one, like Esther." Suddenly he put his arm around her and said, "All right, Sis, we'll do it!"

Leah liked the pressure of his arm around her. She liked the way his teeth flashed white against his tan skin. But she said sharply, "I'm not really your sister, Jeff—we're just pretending!" Somehow the thought of their being just brother and sister disturbed her.

He looked at her, puzzled, and said, "Sure, that's right." Then he said, "Come on, I've got to go tell Tom."

When Tom left the next morning after arguing half the night against the scheme, he had finally given in. "All right, I'll get you some extended leave, even if I have to go to General Jackson. But you watch yourself, you hear me?" Looking over at Leah, he said, "You mind what she tells you. That girl's not only good-looking—she's got a head full of sense."

Tom kissed Leah, shook hands with his brother, and then gave Jeff a hug. "Write as soon as you find out something about Pa."

When Tom had left, Jeff felt a little lonesome and a bit frightened.

They had told her parents and Sarah what they intended to do.

Mr. Carter said, "I guess I'll have to be a part of it. Maybe I can pretend to be an old uncle or something like that. Anyway we're going to get Jeff in to see his daddy—that's the important thing."

"Thank you, Mr. Carter," Jeff said. He looked around and said, simply, "I thank all of you. I don't understand this war—people like us, closer than anybody, yet on different sides."

Mrs. Carter put her arms around him. "It'll be over soon—someday—and then we'll start living again."

Later, Jeff and Leah walked along the road watching the stars, which looked like flickering candles high overhead. They were silent most of the time and then began to talk of how they might get in to see Jeff's father.

Finally, Jeff turned to her and said, "I don't know what I'd do without you, Leah. You're like old Napoleon."

"You mean I'm like a fish?" Leah exclaimed indignantly.

"Oh, shoot, no! I didn't mean that!" Jeff stammered. "I mean like I wanted Napoleon always to be there. Well, when I think about this place—" he hesitated and his voice dropped to a whisper "—I always think about you being here."

Without warning, Leah reached up, pulled his head down, and kissed him.

Jeff blinked. "Best friends, aren't we, Leah?"

Leah looked up at him, took his hand, and led him along the road. "Yes, best friends always, Jeff."

They glanced up as an owl passed over their heads, making a mournful sound. Somehow the cry of the night bird filled Leah with a sense of some sadness that lay ahead.

But she said, "We *are* best friends, Jeff. And whatever is ahead, our best-of-all friend Jesus will make everything right."

Then Leah laughed and pulled at his sleeve. "Come on, let's go home, and I'll make you an apple pie!"

The Bonnets and Bugles Series includes:

- Drummer Boy at Bull Run—#1
- Yankee Belles in Dixie—#2
- The Secret of Richmond Manor—#3
- The Soldier Boy's Discovery—#4
- Blockade Runner—#5
- The Gallant Boys of Gettysburg—#6
- The Battle of Lookout Mountain—#7
- Encounter at Cold Harbor—#8
- Fire Over Atlanta—#9
- Bring the Boys Home—#10